For:

Matthew Curno Crane O'Reilly

(1965–2012)

With love

P. A. Gillis

THE GREAT NEPTUNE BAR MYSTERY

The Mopalot Mysteries of
Aberbryncraig – Book 1

AUSTIN MACAULEY PUBLISHERS™

LONDON • CAMBRIDGE • NEW YORK • SHARJAH

A CIP catalogue record for this title is available from the British Library.

ISBN 9781528994057 (Paperback)
ISBN 9781528994064 (Hardback)
ISBN 9781528994071 (ePub e-book)

www.austinmacauley.com

First Published (2021)
Austin Macauley Publishers Ltd
25 Canada Square
Canary Wharf
London
E14 5LQ

Dai News Fussing in His Shop

Dai News in his shop

'Oh, botheration and penguins!' Dai News says under his breath, 'I think there's one missing again!' It was a Neptune Choc Bar that is missing. Let me tell you about it.

Dai News' Newspaper and Sweetmeats Emporium is about halfway along the High Street in Aberbryncraig by the sea, opposite the *Heddlu* (police) station.

Inside the shop, the proprietor Mr Dafyd Edwards – locally known as Dai News – is frequently found counting his stock.

The newspapers for sale are neatly arranged along his counter in alphabetical order, and in a good place for him to keep an eye on them.

His sweetmeats (sweets and chocolates to you) are all in jars, on the shelf behind him and there are also some under his glass counter. These can only be seen by looking sideways below the newspapers. There is also a second glass display case to Dai's left, standing on top of the counter which is also filled with jars and trays of sweets. Except, that is, for the Neptune Choc Bars – which are delicious – and the Cough Cough Drops, which always brought tears to the eyes of all but the most hardened of fishermen. Both these items arrive at the shop in rather fine display boxes which Dai News can't resist. So, they are carefully placed on top of his second display case at eye level, to attract attention and so that Dai can keep an eye on them while he sells things.

The other item besides the posh display boxes, and again in a rather brightly coloured state, is the Lifeboat collection box. If the Lifeboat box had a Choc Bar on top, it could be mistaken for the Neptune Choc Bar display box, as the latest design was very blue indeed. It is nearly always empty except for a few buttons and maybe a discarded Cough Cough Cough Drop. No one notices that it is a bit heavier than usual just now.

The Cough Cough Cough Drops' box is black and white and has a rather startling aspect to it, besides being very shiny. While the Neptune Choc Bars have a box with various nautical emblems including Neptune himself, a very voluptuous mermaid, a fisherman, and a large boat – looking as if they are made of chocolate. All this, against a tasteless but arresting, fluorescent blue background, quite unsuitable for chocolate bars. Both boxes fold down to display their wares in a most enticing way.

Each Neptune Bar also has an incongruous bright blue wrapper. This has invited comments along the lines that it should be chocolate coloured. However, the manufacturers know what they are doing: Neptune Bars have always stood out.

We already know Dai News places them on eye level, at the top of his glass cabinet, in order to make people notice them, while keeping them within his own line of vision. He also writes down each one sold, in bundles of five marks. One, two, three and four as upright marks, like a fence, and number five being a line across all of them like a belt. This means that he can add them up in fives at the end of the day. This is necessary because of the botheration and penguins. In other words, it is because some are missing. Needless to say, the Cough Cough Cough Drops persistently remain exactly as they are left. No, sorry! Evans the Lifeboat bought some once.

Neptune Choc Bars have a good layer of runny toffee; a thick layer of dark chocolate truffle; a thin, cockled crust of crunchy, nutty stuff; a generous topping of gooey icing; all encased in a marvellous coating of slightly soft, whipped milk chocolate, which melts in your mouth.

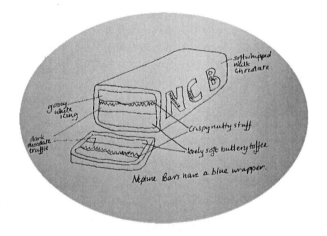

A Neptune Bar

Everyone loves them. Children save up their pocket money for them, old ladies hoard them for grandchildren, themselves, and their fancy old men. The old men have probably already bought them for themselves and have almost certainly eaten them immediately, in the street. Young men do exactly the same. Women get them two at a time, not for the children, but to eat both at once when they get a minute to sit down.

Dai News likes Neptune Choc Bars but he never allows himself to have one; he just counts them obsessively. This is not the only thing Dai News does obsessively. He also counts

9

his sheets, towels and cutlery; weighs all the things in his fridge every day; only has a light on if he is in the room and cleans his shop all the time (though the famous Mrs Mopalot cleans it too). Dai makes more dust than is healthy around the sweets. He also has an elaborate routine of switching off, closing and locking up every time he goes in or out of his flat or shop.

As he counts, (he is counting the Neptune Choc Bars at present) he swears quietly to himself: 'Oh, botheration and penguins!' Dai says for a second time under his breath, 'I think there's one missing again!'

He had, of course, consulted the scrubby bit of paper in his right hand.

'Ten, fifteen, twenty, thirty, thirty-two,' he mutters. 'Thirty-two from fifty,' (Neptune Choc Bar displays were quite large) 'there should be eighteen left.'

He takes all the bars out of the display and lays them on the newspapers. He arranges them in twos. There is one over. He counts: 'Two, four, six, eight, ten, twelve, fourteen, sixteen, SEVENTEEN!'

He pulls at his hair, making it stand out in pleats, and starts jumping up and down. Fortunately, at this moment Mrs Mopalot opens the door. Dai News stands stock still, feeling a bit silly but still says,

'It HAS happened again! That's four gone this week and its only Thursday.'

Mrs Mopalot joins in, 'It is a disgrace, you know, people taking your Neptune Choc Bars from you, Mr Edwards. A disgrace. And it is not even quite summer so there are no visitors to speak of, to blame it on either.'

'One Neptune Bar has gone every day this week!' Dai News mourns.

'I'll put the kettle on,' sympathises Mrs Mopalot.

Now – Aberbryncraig

You need to know more about the seaside village of Aberbryncraig. The name, which translates from the Welsh as "estuary hill rock", includes everything you could wish for to make a place perfect. At least, that's what the people who live there think. Its beside the River Geraint which has its estuary just along the beach; the surrounding high hills are beautiful; and Cigfran rock (which means "raven rock" and there are ravens there, sometimes anyway) is not far away. There is also, of course, the sea, with its long, mostly safe beach (only one person drowned last year) and a coastal walk to the next village Aberspong.

You could also walk to Aberspong along the sands. No translation of "spong" is available; maybe there was a River Spong at one time? Perhaps the Vikings brought the name? Aberspong was much more popular with the visitors at this time, than Aberbryncraig and therefore Aberbryncraigites considered it a terrible place to live.

Aberbryncraig does get some of its own visitors. These come in the school holidays mostly, but that doesn't take into account the legions of caravans in well-hidden sites all around the village. The inhabitants of these caravans are here most of the summer from Easter till November and are counted, more or less tolerantly, as residents. The ones in the static caravans also arrive for Christmas, New Year and bonfire night, so they are considered more residential still and known to give good parties to which everyone is invited.

There was a bit more litter during the summer and a few things disappear without being paid for, but mostly Dai Copper, the local *heddlu* (police) chap has little to do. That didn't mean he is prepared to tackle just about anything, as we will find out.

The beach was never full – being several miles long – so it's always possible to find somewhere to sunbathe in peace. The promenade has been well shored up with strategically placed piles of stones (worked out by computer) to make the best job of keeping the tides in their place, which is in the sea and not on land. In the winter, the tides assail these sea defences with gusto but there have been no floods since the new defences were put in, although the sea always rushes about, gnashing its teeth and making a good effort.

Only the undaunted walk the beach and promenade in the winter, as the waves lashing the shore also soak anyone on foot and you can't hear yourself think for the noise.

Along the High Street though, you could hardly hear the sea – you could be anywhere in Wales.

The High Street is well supplied with shops too: two supermarkets, a hardware shop, a shoe shop, two posh restaurants, a wonderful butcher's, a bread shop that sells delicious honey cakes, a couple of half-hearted souvenir shops, two decent cafés, and the Aberbryncraig Newspaper and Sweetmeats Emporium presided over by Mr Dafyd Edwards, commonly known as Dai News, as you already know. Dai is the fourth Dafyd Edwards to inherit the shop from the original proprietor, his great-great-grandfather: Dafyd Edwards the First.

No one ever uses the full name of the Aberbryncraig Newspaper and Sweetmeats Emporium, of course. They just call it the Emporium. Within the Emporium, Dai News is a bit of an eccentric and you know he does things with obsessive care. Mostly, these things involve counting, weighing and measuring, but more on that later.

Surprisingly few people live in Aberbryncraig; just about enough to keep the school supplied with children. So, news gets around like wildfire and everyone knows all there is to know about everyone else, including the caravan residents. Therefore, it was really strange when no one had any helpful ideas about the disappearing Neptune Chocolate Bars. Of course, everyone knows they *are* disappearing.

Mrs Mopalot

Now, Mrs Mopalot needs some explanation. She's not your ordinary cleaner by any means, but then, she *is* an ordinary cleaner because she cleans. She cleans and cleans and cleans. She cleans for everyone, for Dai News (although she calls him Mr Edwards, as she should), for the vicar (she just calls him Vicar, its simpler) and for Father Umber (she has been known to call him Dad by mistake).

Father Umber has only been in Aberbryncraig for fifty years and is the priest for the Catholic Church just off the High Street (fancy running a *Catholic* church in Wales). I told you Aberbryncraig had everything: the Methodist preacher, the Alternative Methodist preacher, the Baptist Minister, the doctor, the heddlu (police) and lots of other people in bungalows just behind the prom – notably Mr Aled Jones, who is about to be christened Mr Wooly Wobbly by the Aberbryncraig school children. Within the week, he will be Mr Wooly Wobbly to everyone.

Mrs Mopalot's name has an obvious source as she frequently mops. Some people actually call her that – if they are very cheeky or are very close friends – its "Mrs M", in most cases.

Her real name is Branwen Jenkins and she's married to Mr Idwall Jenkins. They are both rotund and very happy, with a partiality for cocoa, especially with a piece of Neptune Bar stirred and melted into it. This delicious habit, of course, helps explain their rotundity.

Mrs M is inquisitive; she pokes her nose into everything. This is partly why she enjoys her job so much. She would never look in drawers or cupboards or anywhere she doesn't have to clean, but her eyes and ears are open all the time and she hoovers up all the information she can. She has always loved a conundrum or mystery and bores Mr Idwall Jenkins stiff with her tales while he tries to read his Railway magazine in bed. He is reputed to have never, ever, finished reading a Railway magazine. No one is quite sure if this is an apocryphal tale though.

Mrs Mopalot is very interested in the disappearing Neptune Choc Bars and of course, she has found out all about them while cleaning for Dai News at the Emporium.

That Evening Mrs Mopalot Confides in Her Husband

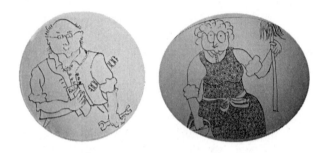

Mr and Mrs Mopalot

Dusk had settled. Mrs Mopalot and her husband Idwall Jenkins (known by everyone, much to his disgust, as "Mr Mopalot") were propped up in bed on a multitude of pillows, with a cup of cocoa on each bedside table.

'Pass me the Railway Modellers magazine, beloved,' requested Mr Jenkins.

'It's not over here,' his wife replied.

'Oh, it's all right beloved; it's under my pillow.'

'Stop wriggling! I'm spilling my cocoa! And believe you me, I had the same problem with Dai News today.'

'You've been drinking cocoa in bed with Dai News, beloved?'

'No, Stoopid! He was counting his Neptune Choc Bars again and he was in such a state that he bumped into me and made me spill my tea.'

'Mrs Jenkins, beloved, why is that man such a fusspot? Every shop loses a few bits and pieces over the year. He should put it down to experience and allow for it in his accounts. Now, let me get on with this article!' (The article was a completely fascinating one about how to make a lump of silver paper and some gluey paint look like a river. Should you be interested in making landscapes for railway models, of course.)

'It's a bit weird though,' Mrs Mopalot went on, 'One Neptune Choc Bar goes missing every day, never more than one, and never a day goes by when one's not pinched.'

'That is a bit strange. He should mount a guard over them. Have a Neptune Bar surveillance team on the go. See if the Chief Constable can do anything about it. Now let me read in peace.'

'I'm going find out what's happening there.'

'Look love, you've got Doc. Watts, all that lot in the sheltered housing, Dai Copper, the Heddlu, Father Umber, the Vicar *and* Dai News plus I don't know how many others to clean for – you haven't got *time* to go sleuthing.'

'We'll see about that,' said Mrs Mopalot firmly.

Children on Their Way to School Talk About Stealing Sweets; Have They Stolen Neptune Choc Bars?

Morgan, Bethan, Owen and Myfanwy.

At exactly eight thirty-three in the morning, Morgan called for his friend Owen so they could walk to school together as usual. There were two girls – Myfanwy and Bethan – not far behind Morgan, and he was ignoring them.

'Girls!' He muttered to himself.

Owen didn't think in the same way, as he has three sisters and is used to girls, even if he does think they are a bit boring. He turned round and smiled. The girls giggled.

They were all heading towards the Emporium and all four wanted to look through the windows at the Neptune Choc Bars perched in prolific gorgeousness on top of the glass cabinet; and also to be slightly embarrassed by the voluptuous chocolate mermaid's appendages on the display box. Dai News didn't put anything in the window to impede anyone's view. This was not only because window dressing was a skill which was beyond him but also because he liked to look out, spotting customers, and sometimes making faces at them, depending on who they were.

So, in full face-making mode, Dai News saw the children outside and glared at them through his window, mouthing "Go away" at them as well. Morgan, feeling belligerent and also hungry, produced a two-penny piece and opened the shop door.

'Can I have a liquorice shoelace please, Mr News?' he asked.

'You cheeky, young scoundrel!' Dai News growled, 'That's no way to address your elders! My name, as you well know, is Edwards. Mr Edwards to you, and I've got a good mind to speak to your father about you!'

Dai held out the sweet a little out of Morgan's reach, while taking the two pence from him. 'Call me by my proper name in future, or I won't serve you.' And then the miserable shopkeeper made him grab ineffectively for the sweet before releasing it.

Back outside on the pavement, Morgan shared the liquorice – not quite fairly – with everyone, even giving both the girls a small piece. Ungratefully, they laughed at him and Morgan blushed to the roots of his hair.

'What do you think of those Neptune Bars?' ventured Myfanwy, 'I love them, but they're fifty pence.' She didn't mention the little secret she had regarding Neptune Choc Bars: she did save up and get one as a gift for a very ungrateful person once. She now wished she had eaten it herself.

'I know, they are utterly splendiferous,' Owen said longingly.

'Oh look, here comes that Mr Jones from the bungalows,' Bethan put in, 'I often see him with a Neptune Bar. I think he has one most days.'

'Lucky blighter!'

'Come on, let's go, we'll be late.' Morgan was feeling responsible now and wanted to put some distance between himself and his embarrassment. Then, he had an idea. 'Hey, what about buying one between us?'

'We could, I suppose,' put in Bethan, 'how much is four into fifty pence?'

Owen was good at Maths. 'Twelve and a half pence,' he said.

'Or, what about nicking one?' Morgan was in with both feet again.

'Would you really do that?' Myfanwy said, not believing that he would.

'If the rest of you distracted the old bloke, I could put one in my pocket when he's not looking.'

'You couldn't reach the top of that cabinet,' Owen said dismissively.

'I could if you gave me a leg up.'

'Stealing's wrong!' Bethan blustered without thinking.

'Trust a girl to spoil it.'

'No, she's not spoiling it. Anything could happen if we were caught.'

'My mum would go mad.'

'And mine.'

'I'd lose my pocket money.'

'I would have to stay in for ages.'

The subject, by common consent, was resolved and dropped.

Mr Jones shimmied past them.

'That old bloke walks like a jelly fish.' Morgan's whisper wasn't quite quiet enough.

'Pysgod Wibly Wobly,' murmured Bethan, who was improving her Welsh. (Pysgod wibly wobly means jellyfish in Welsh, or it does these days anyway.)

'Woolly Wobbly!' Owen put in, 'My granddad says he was always woolly, even at Junior School. He says he couldn't think of two things at once. If he brought his homework, he forgot his dinner money and if he brought his dinner money, he forgot his homework. He was known for it.'

'I like him and his funny walk.'

'Girls!'

'Well, I do and so does Myfanwy, I bet.'

'Yeah, I do but I don't think he likes us, and he can be a very rude man.'

Mr Aled Jones, now with the alias Mr Woolly Wobbly, had turned and put out his tongue at them, followed by a loud raspberry.

The children turned and ran, giggling.

So much for those four children stealing Neptune Bars; not that anyone knew they had rejected the idea. So, they were still suspected. The school was full of others to suspect anyhow. So why worry.

Mr Wooly Wobbly

Then Dai News Finds Three Neptune Bars Missing, Which Makes Things Worse

Not many days later, the walls were vibrating and the glass about to shatter at the Emporium. It was Dai News. He was wailing fit to smash the glass.

Mrs Mopalot arrived to clean. She had had a lovely walk to work. The breeze was light, not like that awful autumn and winter wind which sometimes whistled and screamed through Aberbryncraig (never mind what the season was), and the sun, although watery, was peeping out, so there was little need for a coat. This peaceful beginning to her morning was not destined to last.

The noise, as she opened the door of the Emporium, was such that she shut it again while she gathered up her courage to go in. She wondered if Mr Edwards had finally flipped and she would have to send for the men in the white coats to take him away.

There was a brief lull in the noise so she rushed through the door before he could start again and demanded to know what the matter was. She had to ask him twice before he could trust himself to speak. Then he muttered miserably:

'Oh, Mrs Jenkins, it's awful. There are three Neptune Bars missing this morning and my profits are never going to stand the strain. I might as well give up now and the Edwards' have been here in this shop for five generations! Great-great-granddad will be turning over in his grave! And…and…father will haunt me!' With this awful prediction, he burst into tears.

The situation wasn't helped when young Owen from the school put his head around the door and said, 'Can I have a

Neptune Bar, Mr New—Edwards? Quick, I'm late for school!'

The roar that followed this request caused the youngster to retreat in a hurry, saying to the three other children waiting outside that Dai News was getting pottier day by day.

'I'll go and get it,' said Bethan, 'Give *me* the money.'

As she opened the door, Dai News got ready to give another furious roar, but when he saw the meek, (Bethan was good at looking meek when it suited her) little girl standing in front of him, he didn't.

He only grunted, 'Yes?' and Bethan got her Neptune Bar, having said 'please' like a good girl, and in just the right obsequious tone of voice.

As she left the shop, she whispered to Mrs Mopalot,

'What's the matter with Mr Edwards?'

So Mrs Mopalot told her, which meant that the whole village knew by eleven that night. The children told other children in the playground. All of those children told their parents. All the parents told every one of their friends, over the fence and on the telephone. The village telegraph worked its usual magic and made Dai News' distress common knowledge. Most people suggested that he was potty, just as Owen had.

Mrs Mopalot managed to calm Dai News down and made him a cup of tea, which she served him in his sitting room. Of course, she had to say she would look after the shop while she was cleaning and would keep a strict eye on the Neptune Bars. She did this willingly, to keep Dai News out of the way for a bit. Mrs Mopalot managed to clean the glass while Dai was drinking his tea, for which she was very thankful.

When he came back, Mrs M insisted on learning Dai News' method of checking his sales of Neptune Bars and counting the ones left. When this had been explained, they religiously checked and counted again. Twice. It was obvious that there were three missing. Mrs M suggested Dai get another cup of tea while she finished cleaning, to keep him out of the way again, of course. She had hoped she'd get the floor done before he came back.

Mrs M fetched her broom and mop, filling the bucket with water, soap flakes and bleach on the way. She started to sweep, which is what she did first. She always started from the inside and worked her way towards the door because she swept the dust out of the door when she got to it. Not what the street sweepers liked, but she had always done it that way. It was a naughty thing to do, but it made life easier.

As Mrs M shoved her broom under the counter, she heard a rustle. Dai News was rarely untidy so she assumed he had dropped one of his bits of counting paper. She got her broom behind the annoying crinkle and swept it towards herself. It appeared. She gasped.

It was two Neptune Choc Bars; dusty, but still safely in their wrappers.

'Dai!' she yelled, completely forgetting that she always called him 'Mr Edwards' respectfully, 'I've found your Choc Bars!'

However, when he looked at them, Dai only said miserably, 'But there's still the one missing.'

Mrs Mopalot wondered if she might find other choc bars around the shop, not "taken", but rather "lost" by Dai himself.

No one bothered to tell the village telegraph that two had turned up. Not that it would have helped Dai News' reputation anyway.

Mrs Mopalot Tells Mr Mopalot as She Always Does

The Mopalot bedroom crackled with tension. Mr Mopalot had put his magazine down and was making a dive for Mrs Mopalot with an intention to tickle while Mrs Mopalot was frustrating this aim because she wanted to relate the story about Dai News losing three Neptune Choc Bars and wailing. The ensuing struggle nearly unseated a cocoa, and in the end, Mrs Mopalot gave in. With some pleasure.

After a while, she got her wish to tell the gossip. Mr M went downstairs to make replacement cocoa for the ones that had gone cold.

When he got back, Mrs M explained that there had been a hysterical outpouring from Mr Edwards at the Emporium, 'He thought he'd had *three* Neptune Bars stolen, you see.'

'Yes, beloved,' said her husband, 'I know. Owen's mum told me. They all say he's potty.'

'Well, this time, I found two of the Bars.'

'Owen's mum didn't know any had been found. Perhaps Dai News loses all the ones he goes on about! Perhaps he's just inefficient? What do you think, beloved?'

'Not with his way of counting everything. You know he weighs everything in his fridge every day?'

'No, I didn't know that. He must be mad. Or do you think he's got an obscure sort of medical syndrome? A chocolate bar fetish? An anti-theft worriment? He doesn't sound like someone who could *lose* a Neptune Bar every day on his own, though. Do you think he's eating them and saying nothing? Pretending they've been stolen?'

'I wouldn't think so. He writes down everything he has from the shop and puts the money in the till at the end of the day.'

'Not very likely then. I give up. Hey, come here you!' And Mr Jenkins made another grab for his wife with disastrous results for the new cocoas.

Dai News Cracks

The next Thursday evening, Dai News shuffled around his little newsagents and sweet shop as he did every day of his narrow, bad-tempered life. He ended up facing the ornate and startlingly bright display box containing the diminishing Neptune Choc Bars. Clutched in his small, mean fist, was the tally of his sales of these bars, that he made every day of his life. There were five lots of four vertical lines with a line through them on his paper, each representing five bars – that made twenty Neptune Choc Bars sold that day. He laboriously counted the remaining bars in the box. There was one missing. Of course, there was. There always was.

Swearing horribly, but under his breath so that Mrs Mopalot would not hear, as she was still cleaning the glass front of the counter, Dai News shuffled back behind it again.

'Lost one again, Dai?' Mrs M asked sympathetically.

'Do you know I have? But of course, you know! I don't suppose you've had one yourself?'

'Mr Edwards!' exclaimed Mrs Mopalot, shocked. 'You know I have! I had two; one for me and one for Mr Jenkins, and I gave you a pound coin for them, as you are very well aware!'

Dai News shrank visibly under Mrs Mopalot's ire. She pursued her point 'You know I would no more take a Neptune Bar and not pay for it than fly in the air! I am mortally offended and I may as well tender my resignation and leave you to the mercies of Fanny Williams!' She threw down her mop.

As Mrs M threatened to leave quite frequently, but never went, this did not really bother Dai News, but the thought of Fanny Williams did. The lady was well-known; both for her shady morals and her inefficient use of a mop. She never did the corners. Dai didn't want to be left to mop for himself, (he had an aversion to wet cleaning) in order to make sure it was all done.

'Oh, Mrs M,' he wheedled, 'I didn't mean it! I was only incensed. I don't know what to do, I really don't. I can't cope. It's causing me to lose sleep. I don't know how long I can go on,' he paused and thought for a minute, then asked, 'What do you think I should do?'

Apart from shutting up about it? thought Mrs Mopalot, but she said, comfortingly and forgivingly, 'I tell you what, Mr Edwards, why don't you have a word with Dai Copper, sorry, I mean Constable Watkins at the Heddlu? He might have some good ideas.'

Dai News let out a wisp of a smile.

'Perhaps I might,' he said, and was comforted.

Mr Mopalot Finds Out That Dai News Is Going to the Police

Mr and Mrs Mopalot were comfortably ensconced in their feather-pillowed, snuggly bed, contemplating their cocoas when Mrs Mopalot remembered something, 'Idwall dear, I must pop downstairs for a moment. I have a surprise for you. Put your cocoa down while I get out of bed – we don't want a repeat of yesterday's cocoa fountain, do we?'

This tactless reference was referring to a gargantuan shuffle made by Mr Mopalot on the previous evening – as he made a grab for Mrs Mopalot – which had caused an entire mug of cocoa to be sent flying in the air. It had rained down on the bed, covering most of it. The memory made him wince, but he said nothing, putting his cocoa down carefully.

'It took me three hours to wash all that lot and I was late for Dai News and Mr Jones...' Mrs Mopalot's voice faded into the distance as she descended the stairs.

She returned quickly, carrying two Neptune Choc Bars.

'Ooooh!' groaned Mr M, 'What a treat! I should have bought those, beloved, to make up for the cocoa. I am so very sorry about that, only, I had an itch on my bum and I just had to scratch it...'

Huh, thought Mrs M. Pull the other one – I know what you were up to!

'Enough, Stoopid. I forgive you,' she said and thought fondly of the gales of laughter which had followed the accident, and the damp snuggles and cuddles which had come later and the fact that the next morning there had been some cocoa in surprising places.

As they devoured their treats, Mrs Mopalot began the saga of Dai News' loss of another Neptune Bar. Mr Mopalot composed his face to think of something else and not look bored.

'And he had the cheek to ask if I'd had it!!!'

That brought Mr M back to the present:

'Oh, beloved, I expect he was pulling your leg.'

'No, he wasn't. He was being nasty. I had to say I would leave him to Fanny Williams in the end, and I would too.'

'No, you wouldn't. That woman is a real muck worm and useless as a cleaner and well you know it.'

'I do but it would serve him right. Any way, he moaned so much I told him to go to see Dai Copper about it!'

This was too much for her husband, who began to shriek with laughter. Between splutters, he gasped, 'I'd give anything to be a fly on the wall and hear what Dai Copper has to say about that!'

'So would I.'

'I think you're a wicked woman.'

'I might be.'

These remarks nearly caused another cocoa fall, but it was just avoided in time as Mr Mopalot demonstrated just how wicked he hoped Mrs Mopalot might be.

Dai News Visits the Heddlu

Dai Copper was filling in his timesheets, when Mrs Mopalot peeped round the door of the station. He put down his pen with relief and looked up in surprise.

'Hello Mrs M,' he said, 'It's not Thursday, is it? I've been doing paperwork and it always confuses me. Come along in. The staff kitchen's a mess, I'm afraid, but I forgot you were coming, so I haven't tidied it.'

'I'm not here on business, constable. It's not Thursday until the day after tomorrow,' said Mrs Mopalot, putting him right and inadvertently telling Constable Watkins what was wrong with his timesheets.

'Oh, what is it then? Nothing serious, I hope?'

'I hope so, too,' she said, stifling a giggle, 'I ought to warn you that Dai News is coming over to report the loss of a Neptune Choc Bar or two, and the news got around.'

'Good gracious!'

She waited for a moment, then added,

'There's quite a crowd outside.'

'Flip,' said the harassed policeman.

'I'd stay and listen, but I'm late for the Vicar, and with this, a cowardly Mrs M backed out of the door again, but she didn't go away.

Dai Copper heard her say,

'I wish you the best of luck Mr Edwards,' as the door was held open and Dai News grumbled his way in. There was a suppressed snorty laughter from outside, because of the village telegraph working again and the resultant crowd finding it impossible to contain their mirth.

'Can I help you, sir?' Dai Copper's tone was formal.

'I certainly hope you can,' began Dai News, 'I've had fifty, FIFTY Neptune Choc Bars, at fifty pence each, I tell you, stolen from my shop! I tell you, that's TWENTY-FIVE POUNDS worth of chocolate. I can't afford it, I tell you!'

Dai Copper composed his face into an expression of sympathy and tried to look serious as he said,

'That's quite a lot of chocolate, Mr Edwards, can you give me an idea of how bulky that might be in total?'

'It isn't bulky in total!' snapped the impatient shopkeeper, 'they go one at a time! Anyone could pop one in their pocket!'

'So, how long has this been going on for?' The policeman pressed his lips firmly together.

'50 days. One a day.' Dai News' tone seemed suitable for speaking to a small child.

'And Sundays?'

'And Sundays.'

Maths wasn't Dai Copper's strong point, as was demonstrated by his timesheets, but he did his best to divide seven into fifty, failed and looked puzzled.

'Seven weeks and one day!' growled Dai News, who knew what he was trying to work out. 'Well, what are you going to do about it?'

'I can suggest a few things.'

'Go on.'

'Firstly, have a "one child at a time" policy in the shop. I can give you a poster about that.'

'I don't think the children can reach that high.'

'You'd be surprised how high children can reach. Any way, they can give each other a leg up.'

'I think it must be an adult.'

'Have a "one adult at a time" policy.'

There was suppressed laughter from outside, along with whispers.

'Okay then, what else?'

Dai Copper knew about Neptune Bars and had bought one or two. Most of the villagers had. He knew where they were displayed.

'Why don't you put them in a glass case?' he suggested.

'Then I wouldn't sell so many,' said Dai News, 'people like the display box. It's a good display box. They help themselves. I don't mind when they pay for them. I sell lots. It's only this one person, the one who takes a Neptune Bar every day!'

'It could be a gang.' The policeman was in danger of losing control here. He went on with some difficulty, 'I know! You could always get some CCTV.'

'That stuff's expensive.'

'It would pay for itself in the end,' Dai Copper said, adding under his breath, 'But not at seven Neptune Bars a week.'

By this time, the policeman was having great difficulty containing his giggles, especially since he could see some of the crowd outside the frosted window and quite a few ears pressed against it, distorted by the glass.

'Can't you investigate it?' Dai News pleaded.

Dai Copper couldn't resist: 'I don't think the "Serious Crime Squad" can fit it in just at the moment, sir.'

As he was now stretched to his limit, he rushed to the kitchen, making strangled sounds, as the laughter from outside rose to a crescendo.

Dai News gave up and hurried to the door. People scattered as quickly as they could.

'You're all heartless!' he shouted after them, 'wait until you want a Neptune Bar and they've all been nicked!'

Later, Mrs Mopalot Regrets Laughing at Dai News

The Mopalots were squirrelled under the coverlet, as it was a cold night and Mr Mopalot had inadvertently switched off the central heating for several hours, instead of turning it up, as he should have done. They allowed the odd hand to reach out carefully for cocoa, and then the usual Mopalot bedtime conversation happened.

Mrs M began: 'You know love, I feel bad about all that pother with Dai News today.'

'What pother, beloved?'

'When he went to see Dai Copper.'

'I didn't realise he'd actually *gone*.'

'How did you miss it? I was sure someone would have told you. I said he was going myself. Everyone and his dog were there. They were all listening at the window. Some of them even put their ears against the glass.'

'I was working in Aberspong, beloved, and I'm sorry you feel bad, but I do hope that won't stop you telling me what Dai Copper said.'

'Of course, it won't. He said he didn't think the "Serious Crime Squad" could fit it in just at the moment—' she was interrupted by squawks of laughter from Mr Mopalot, so she became a bit louder so he could laugh and hear, 'and then, Dai Copper had to rush to the kitchen,' she almost shouted, 'because he couldn't keep his face straight any longer, and neither could anybody outside the window; they all howled with laughter, and Dai News came out and yelled at them all. Well, at us all I suppose, because I did it too.' The last bit came out in a rush and she burst into tears, silencing Mr Mopalot's laughter at a blow.

Taking her in his chubby little arms and stroking her hair, Mr Mopalot tried to calm her down.

OK beloved,' he said gently 'perhaps you had better do a bit of investigating then. See if you can find out what's happening here.'

She replied, 'Oh Stoopid!'

He kissed her on the top of her head and pulled her under the bedclothes.

So that's how Mrs Mopalot's investigations began.

First clue: The Vicar's Sermon

It was a quiet Sunday morning at Saint Carresvan's – the solid, ancient, Anglican (sorry, High Welsh) church in Aberbryncraig. The congregation was big enough but considering the population of the village, not that good. Of course, there were several, oh alright many, other calls to the faithful on Sunday mornings. There was the very small number congregating at Saint Neeps (only two, as it was the Catholic one), and some more at the Methodists and the Alternative Methodists, with the Baptists claiming quite a few, but it couldn't have been a good turnout anywhere. There weren't enough souls to go round.

Mrs Mopalot didn't often go to church. Well, she went about once a month to support the vicar. This particular Sunday she felt she should go and ask the Almighty about the best way to proceed with her investigations.

Chatting with Him as she should: on her knees while the vicar intoned completely unrelated prayers, she didn't seem to get very far at all, and was still confused. She did have a second word "upstairs", as she called talking to God – during one of the psalms – but felt it didn't go anywhere either and there was certainly no answer. Or if there was one, she didn't hear it. Sometimes, God answered prayers in unusual ways, she knew, so she didn't despair.

Then it happened.

After the hymn, when the collection was taken – the number of buttons in the collection plate reminding her of the lifeboat collection box – the vicar ascended to the pulpit. The congregation settled itself down to sleep, as did Mrs M. She was shaken awake after about three quarters of an hour as the reverend's next words assaulted her ears:

'Neptune Bars,' confessed the vicar, 'You see, I am also subject to the sin of greed. I have a terrible sweet tooth and I am always thinking of the wonderful Neptune Choc Bars that Mr Edwards has in his Emporium. I lust after them.'

Mrs Mopalot gasped, as did one or two others. Was this the answer to her prayer? The vicar went on:

'In the names of the Father, and of the Son and of the Holy Spirit. Amen.' Just when they wanted to know more, he finished! Mrs Mopalot wished she had listened to the rest of the vicar's sermon then, especially as her enquiries in the churchyard later, about what else the Vicar had said, drew a complete blank. Except for Fanny Williams, who said she thought it had been about greed, and that he had been looking right at her all through it!

That much was obvious. Both the subject, and looking at Fanny, who was wearing an almost see through shocking pink dress although it was so cold, she was mostly just showing goose bumps.

Several members of the congregation set off for the Bryn Arms – across the road from the church – for their Sunday morning, post service pint, accompanied by Fanny Williams, who just wanted to get warm.

Mrs M rushed home to get the dinner on and tell Idwall what had happened but was pretty sure he would pour cold water on the idea that the vicar was the Neptune Bar thief. Still, it was exciting just the same and a start to her investigations.

Fanny Williams

Of Course Mr Mopalot Pours Scorn on the Vicar's Confession

Mrs Mopalot put down the potato peeler and turned to confront her husband.

'Idwall Jenkins!' she began dramatically, 'I have a clue about the thefts from Dai News' shop!'

Mr Mopalot tried to arrange a suitable expression on his face, failed, gave up, and left in place the usual sceptical one.

'Yes beloved?' he said, giving up hope.

'Well,' she went on, 'you know how I've been to church this morning…' Mr Mopalot nodded. 'Well, the Vicar gave himself away – in his sermon, if you please!'

'Good grief! Whatever did he say?' Mr Mopalot's imagination was running amok, and on untrammelled lines as well.

'He said he's got a sweet tooth!' Mrs M was triumphant. Mr M's face fell.

'Beloved,' he said patiently, 'That's not evidence. Any number of people who have a sweet tooth satisfy their cravings,' and here, his mind wandered a little again, 'without resorting to stealing a Neptune Choc Bar or any other sort of bar. Most people settle for more jam on their toast, or more sugar in their tea.'

'He did say he lusted after Neptune Bars though. He did actually mention them by name.'

The word "lusted" didn't help Mr M in his attempt to get his thoughts on a proper wavelength. With super-human effort, he sat himself down to get his boots off and tried to make his wife see sense,

'Beloved, get your feet on the ground. You are going off on tangents that will get you nowhere. You need some hard evidence, like seeing someone *taking* one of the bars, or someone else *telling* you they've seen someone taking one, or Mr Edwards saying he's counted them wrong. You can't suspect the dear vicar just because he likes the pothering things! *Everyone* likes the pothering things!'

'Oh, all right, that's a good point,' she sighed, then went on, 'perhaps I've got too involved in this. Maybe I'm being ridiculous, seeing a clue where there isn't one? Perhaps I should back off now and come back to it later?'

'Well, no, I don't think you should, beloved, because I've had another thought and it's a more serious one.'

'What thought?'

'Perhaps, someone is trying to drive Dai News a bit potty; trying to make fun of him.'

'That's awful.'

'It does sound rather farfetched, I know.'

'I hope it is. Whoever would want to have a go at Dai News?'

'Nearly everyone, I should think.'

'Oh no, don't say that. He can be irritating but there's no reason to try and make him worse, and there's no reason to steal to do it!'

'I'm also thinking it would take more than one person to pull it off.'

'A plot, you mean.'

'Yes, a plot.'

Mr and Mrs Mopalot stared at each other in horror.

Seriously disturbed by the thought that some people could be spiteful to Dai News, Mrs Mopalot suggested going and having a chat with Dai Copper, but Mr M was uncertain about the wisdom in this. Did the 'Serous Crime Squad' deal with spiteful bullying they thought. Probably not. It was all very worrying and confusing.

Mrs M Sees the Doctor Eating a Neptune Bar *Twice*

Doc Watts

At nine thirty sharp on Monday, Mrs Mopalot arrived at the Doctor's ready to do a bit of cleaning as usual. Mrs Watts, the doctor's wife, let her in of course.

'Would you start in the surgery, like you always do, please, Mrs Jenkins?' The doctor was a man of habit and called out the same thing from the kitchen every Monday morning, come rain (the frequent weather) or shine. 'I'm doing surgery at ten, so you should be able to give it a go round before then?'

The doctor appeared from his breakfast with a piece of toast between his teeth and a Neptune Bar in his hand. The toast didn't last long and neither did the Neptune Bar. Chobble...chobble...chobble.

Mrs Mopalot had never seen anyone eat a Neptune Bar for breakfast before. In the Mopalot household, chocolate was allowed for breakfast but only occasionally, on a person's birthday, but never something as over the top as a gooey Neptune Bar.

Fascinated, she watched for as long as she felt she politely could, managing to stay and see the last of the chocolate being pushed hurriedly into the doctor's mouth as his wife came into the hall. Then she set off to start cleaning the surgery stifling a giggle.

In the surgery, under a pile of papers, which she felt she *had* to move slightly to dust the doctor's desk, there was another Neptune Bar. This one had a bite out of it and the wrapper was missing. It had melted slightly and the papers were chocolaty. Mrs Mopalot's interest was aroused, although quite why – she wasn't sure.

She didn't mean to look in the drawer, but it was partly open and she couldn't help it, could she? Inside there were rather a lot of Neptune Bars arranged neatly in rows. So neatly, that one wondered if there were some others neatly arranged underneath.

Next, she went to start on the kitchen and met the doctor who passed her on his way out, as she came in. He was holding something furtively. He had pushed it partly up his sleeve but it looked like a familiar blue wrapper. What was going on? Were there Neptune Bars everywhere in this house? She wondered why she hadn't noticed it before and if it had come on suddenly?

Maybe she could pass this on to Mr Mopalot over cocoa? She decided not to. Mr Mopalot had had quite a lot to say about hare-brained theories lately and it might be odd, but it wasn't evidence of theft to have a lot of something – was it?

Just then, Mrs Doctor waltzed into the kitchen enquiring if Mrs Mopalot would like a cup of coffee. Amidst other chatter, she got off her chest the difficulties of making one's husband diet when he spent half his time in the Bryn with those boozy clerics and the rest of his time eating Neptune Bars.

'He's only taken the blasted bars up because I'm trying to get him to lose some weight!' she moaned.

Case solved.

It might amuse Stoopid though, so long as it isn't presented as evidence, Mrs Mopalot thought.

Mr and Mrs Mopalot in Bed Again

Mrs Mopalot snuggled into her fluffy Winceyette nightie; Mr Mopalot had bought it for her last year when she was in bed with a nasty cough. Ooooh, it was warm. Not glamorous, but Mr M didn't seem to mind. He was maybe thinking of what lay was beneath the winceyette surface.

Of course, being in bed, Mr M was well into an article in his *Railway News* about how to wire up a particularly difficult junction on a railway model, and he didn't want to be disturbed.

Mrs Mopalot said, 'I had a fun time at Doctor Watts' today.'

Silence.

'When I was cleaning at Doctor and Mrs Watts' today, I made a surprising discovery. You'd be amazed. I was.'

Nothing.

So, she looked at her spouse. She hadn't for a while, what with them both facing forwards in the bed, she never noticed him much; only when he grabbed her. Mr Mopalot had dropped off to sleep. This caused Mrs Mopalot to bounce up and down. Not to wake him up, you understand, but to get comfortable. Mr Mopalot grunted, then grunted again, louder, then swore quietly. He said,

'What the potheration is going on? I wasn't potheratingly asleep, Branywn. Can't you keep still, beloved? Oh pother, I've dropped my magazine on the floor and it's landed in the po.'

Now, Mr and Mrs Mopalot didn't have a chamber pot under their bed because they still had the outside privy and didn't want to go outside in the night; they had it, because they *used* to have an outside loo and they kept the po out of habit. That meant that there wasn't anything nefarious in the porcelain, but there was still a taboo against dropping anything into it. This taboo was caused by a semiconscious memory of schoolbooks and precious comics covered in wee. Mr M got out of bed to retrieve his magazine, and looked at it carefully, again out of habit.

Mrs Mopalot saw her chance, and said,

'It was weird at Doc Watts' today, Stoop.'

Fighting back a cloud of sleep that threatened to engulf him, Stoop said, as he climbed back into bed, keeping his eyes open with difficulty,

'Tell me what was weird at the doc's, beloved?'

'I think he's got a Neptune Bar fetish!'

'What's a Neptune Bar fetish, beloved? Has he been kissing them?'

They both giggled at this, and Mrs M elaborated, 'the doc was eating one for breakfast, he had one up his sleeve for later, he had a half-eaten one under his papers on his desk, getting his papers all chocolaty and he has a stash of about thirty in a drawer in his desk!' she paused for breath, 'at first, I wondered if he was Dai News' thief. Then I thought you would pour cold water on that one.'

'Possessing Neptune Bars does not mean you have nicked them, beloved. Doc Watts is a rich man and he has the means to buy lots and lots of Neptune Bars if he wants to.'

'I knew you'd say that, so I gave up the idea. But I do think he might be addicted to them. Do you think he should go to Neptune Bars Anonymous?' This was followed by giggles as they both imagined such an organisation and people confessing to being – a what? A neptuneabaraholic? Brilliant. Most of Aberbryncraig would probably have to go.

Mrs Mopalot went on, 'The best was, though, Mrs Watts came into the kitchen to find out if I wanted a cup of coffee – to see if I would make her one, more like – and she was really cross with him, otherwise I don't think she would have said what she did say.'

'Which was?' Mr Mopalot was on automatic as his head was back in his magazine.

'She's got him on a diet and it hasn't a chance of working because he keeps going to the Bryn with the vicar and Father Umber and eating Neptune Bars by the ton. She thinks he's only taken up eating them to spite her because she's trying to get him to lose weight.'

'Not the most brilliant things to combine beer and chocolate,' put in Mr Mopalot, considering the matter, 'I've seen him doing it too. In the Bryn. It made me feel a touch queasy I must say.' And with this, he lunged at Mrs Mopalot and tickled her until she was helpless, leaving his railway magazine to fly in the air and land back in the empty po.

Mr Aled Jones and the Fifty Pence

Mr Aled (Woolly Wobbly) Jones of the jellyfish walk was late in getting up from his comfortable, fluffy, down duvet and bed with its special soft mattress. He wasn't lazy, he was worried. You see he hadn't got a 50 pence piece.

He had searched every pocket and his purse the night before, especially the back pockets of all his trousers as that's where he liked to keep his 50ps. He had looked in the wine glass with the plastic bag stuffed in the top and he had looked in the old spectacles case under his pillow. He had looked everywhere. There was no 50p to be found.

He was late leaving his bed because he had been up for most of the night, looking. Looking for a 50p piece.

He pulled his warm, plaid dressing gown with its twisted cord – with tassels on the ends –round himself and tied it up tight. It was chilly. Then he heard the doorbell, swiftly followed by a key in the lock.

Mrs Mopalot! Hurrah. She would scold him for not being dressed but she might have a 50p! He jelly-fished himself into the hall.

Mrs Mopalot was startled.

'Look at you!' she started, 'Go into that bedroom of yours and put some clothes on, quick, sharp! I'm not here to clean for people who are *dishabilled*!' And with that, she flounced into the kitchen and a smell of bleach and sounds of crashing crockery filled the bungalow.

As soon as he'd, very quickly, finished dealing with his *dishabilled* state (putting on some trousers and a jumper on top of his pyjamas) Mr Jones jelly-fished into the kitchen and asked his important question,

'Have you got a 50p piece Mrs Jenkins?' Then he added, 'Please?' In case that made a difference.

Mrs Mopalot was astounded by his courtesy and realised that it indicated the importance of the occasion and the importance of the request. Mr Jones almost invariably called her Mrs Mopalot to her face, as did certain of the other less sensitive villagers and her very close friends. He simply never called her by her name in that respectful way. It wasn't that he was a rude man; he just had difficulty in holding more than one idea in his head at once. He had been known for it all his life from when he was at school and could only remember his homework OR his dinner money in the morning, as Mrs Mopalot's mother always said.

'Look, I've made you a cup of tea. You sit down and drink it while I go and see if I've got a 50p piece in my bag.' Mrs M said and bustled out wondering why he was in need of a 50p so urgently. He didn't have an electricity meter, in fact she couldn't think of any other immediate use for a 50p piece except for the slot machine in the loos at the Bryn Arms pub, and she didn't think Mr Aled Jones would want any of *those* things. The idea amused her, though, as she searched her purse.

'Here you are, Mr Jones,' she said, finding one, 'and what do you want it for? If you want to tell me, that is?'

His face shining with a pleased look, he answered, 'Oh it's for Dai News. You know, the shop.' as he gave her ten 5ps and jellyfish-walked into his sitting room with his tea.

Wondering what Dai News wanted 50ps for, Mrs Mopalot got on with her chores, but something stuck in her memory, and niggled at her.

Mrs Mopalot Reports to Mr Mopalot the Need Mr Aled Jones Has for Fifty Pence

Mrs and Mr Mopalot were having a good time among pillows, their pretty counterpane, some delicious cocoa, a railway magazine and each other.

Coming up for air and cocoa, Mrs Mopalot remembered something she wanted to say,

'You know, it was a trifle odd this morning at Mr Jones's.'

Mr Mopalot also fancied a little cocoa, especially as this particular mug of cocoa has a large slice of a Neptune Choc Bar melted in it, so he put in conversationally,

'What was odd, beloved?'

'Mr Jones.'

'Mr Jones, if you mean the same one who lives in the bungalows that the children call Mr Woolly Wobbly,' (word gets round like wildfire in Aberbryncraig, even though the children only christened him that last week) 'he's always been odd. Since he was in the Juniors' if my dad's to be believed. Nothing new there.'

'There is. This morning he was desperate for a fifty pence piece. I offered him two twenties and a ten, but that wouldn't do, it had to be a proper fifty.'

'Has he got a meter, for his gas and electric, like?'

'No, and I should know. I've been cleaning for him long enough.'

'What else can you use a fifty pence piece for, beloved? Surely he isn't getting things from the Gents at the Bryn at his age.'

'And at half past nine in the morning, as well!'

'Shocking, beloved,' said Mr Mopalot, and had a good try at getting Mrs Mopalot back under the coverlet. She resisted.

'He was really frantic, and when I eventually found him a 50p, he was so grateful it was pathetic.'

'Didn't you ask him what it was for?'

'I did, sort of, and he said it was for Dai News.'

'Perhaps Dai News is starting to get out a bit more!'

'But surely, he'd go to the chemist's, wouldn't he?'

'Beloved, you're a bandit!' stated her enthusiastic spouse, and this time she did disappear under the covers.

Father Umber's Fictitious Morning in the Priestly Half of the Confessional

Father Umber and The Vicar

The news, or rather the rumour, got round like wildfire again. There seemed to be several sources of rather dubious information but everyone was aware – although no one dared say – it was Mrs Mopalot who started it. She was able to go everywhere, for sure, because she cleaned everywhere. Especially since she worked for all the clerics with whom Aberbryncraig was so liberally endowed, she was the source of all the information. It must be her.

Father Umber was from the Catholic branch of the population and there weren't many of those so Mrs Mopalot was one of the few who saw him frequently. Apart, that is, from his drinking mates in the Bryn. Mrs M's closeness to Father Umber was resented by the Catholic Church attendees.

Both of them. Especially when the content of the rumour was related to them.

You do know, or you might have worked it out, that everyone, absolutely everyone, knew about the Great Neptune Choc Bar Mystery. After Dai News' trip to the *Heddlu*, the secret was completely out. All the children on their way to and from *ysgol* (school) could talk about nothing else. All the old men, while they ate their Neptune Bars in the street, discussed theories amongst themselves.

They annoyed Dai News while paying in the Emporium by never failing to say: "Note down that I'm paying for this now, Dai!" until he was in danger of screaming. All the young mothers and shopkeepers gossiped continuously, and the clerical community had begun praying about the matter. Whether this was in order to enlist the Almighty's help to find the culprit or to shut their congregation and Dai News (who never went to church but did whine to *everyone)* up, it wasn't clear. Everyone was impressed though.

It was this involvement with religion that caused the problem.

The rumour was that someone had been to confessional and had confessed to taking the Neptune Choc Bars, thereby giving Father Umber from Saint Neeps a terrible problem. Of course, he had to respect the confessional and couldn't expose the culprit. Oops.

The fact was that this was eyewash. No one had been to confessional for years, not owing to there being nothing to confess, because there was a ton to confess. It was simply because of the Aberbryncraig lazy gene or possibly the fact that it didn't occur to anyone to go. Father Umber's congregation was small, sometimes only two or three, as has been said before, (somewhat inaccurately), but his church was tiny and beautiful so it was often full of non-praying visitors, which wasn't the comfort it might have been to the cleric.

The poor man was the last to know about all this. The vicar told him in the end, to circumvent the possibility of anyone else doing so. It wasn't an easy encounter, but then, perhaps it was. It certainly had a pleasant finale. Father Umber found it amusing at first and gave a great belly laugh, but on reflection, he was alarmed. It seemed to highlight a failure in the confessional department. The conversation went like this:

Vicar: 'Sorry old man, I didn't want to be the bearer of bad tidings, but it seemed it was my duty to let you know what's going on.'

Father Umber: (recovering from his enormous belly laugh and trying to stop giggling) 'Not exactly bad tidings Vic. Just a touch embarrassing. Could come in handy though, there's not much confessing that goes on in Saint Neeps, you know, and this might start them off, if only to see who else is there in case it's the renowned Choc Bar thief!' and off he went into giggles again.

Vicar: 'Brownie, you're terrible!'

Father Umber: 'I hope I'm right, and it isn't something sinful I'm doing.'

Vicar: 'You mean hoping they'll come to service out of curiosity?'

Father Umber: 'Well, it is a bit sneaky.'

Vicar: 'Don't give it a second thought. There's always a problem getting a good congregation in a little place like this with so much competition for souls. Just make sure they know confession is after the service!'

Father Umber: 'You devious blighter!'

Vicar: 'You have to be.'

He thought for a moment, then added: 'Before the service might be more effective, and don't nick any of mine while you're at it!'

They were about to part on good terms when it occurred to them to go to the Bryn for convivial a pint. So they did.

Come Sunday, the Vicar's congregation (and everyone else's) was minimal and the one at Saint Neeps was huge. The queue for confession contained not only Catholics, but High Welsh, Methodists, Baptists and Alternative Methodists (but not many of those) and nearly encircled the tiny church. Being as almost the whole town was there, no one really discovered anything, (and no one thought for a moment that there was nothing to discover) and they did have to sit through a very long sermon of Father Umber's. He had a wonderful time preaching to such a large congregation. He thanked God later for Neptune Choc Bar thieves, wondering if it was OK to thank Him for this, or if maybe it was a sort of a sin.

Mrs Mopalot Fears She Started the Rumour (Everyone Knows She Did)

It was cocoa time again and Mrs Mopalot was down in the dumps. Mr Mopalot (alias: Idwall Jenkins) hadn't noticed and was having a good time (for once) with his *Railway Modellers Journal*. Mr Mopalot loved reading about model railways and going to exhibitions to look at models other people had made. He knew an amazing amount about the construction and electrical circuits these models had and he was in the process of making a model himself –of the station at Aberbryncraig, of course. During the previous year, he had added two pieces of track to this and made a wiring diagram. Mrs Mopalot had long ago stopped holding her breath for it to be working as had their once hopeful children, grandchildren, nephews and nieces.

As her moping was not observed, Mrs M put down her cocoa mug and wriggled under the blankets with a loud sniff. This alerted Mr M who dragged his eyes from an enticing model engine which had a real, or sort of real, steam coming out of its funnel and said, 'Are you going down with a cold, beloved?'

'NO!'

Realising this was more temper than germs, Mr M put down his magazine regretfully, and turned to his wife. Temper at bedtime bode no good and certainly no sleep.

'Whatever is the matter?' he said, 'are you crying under the bedclothes there?'

'NO!'

'Yes, you are, now come here and tell me all about it.' And with this Mr Mopalot gathered his beloved into his arms and began stroking her hair.

'Oh, Idwall, I've taken it all too far!' Seriously alarmed by the fact that she called him Idwall and not Stoopid, as she usually did, Mr Mopalot upped the stroking and did his best to get to the bottom of the problem.

'Would you like some more cocoa, beloved? Might that cheer you up? Or do you want to tell me all about it?' The stroking became rather frantic.

'Oh, Idwall, leave my hair alone for a minute and let me sit up. I was so lonely here with you buried in that magazine, and I feel such a fool.'

'Come on, then. I'll help you sit up and you tell me about it. *Then* I'll make some more cocoa.' With this, he hauled his wife into a sitting position and patted her into place.

She began,

'You know all that fuss at Saint Neeps last Sunday?'

'It was a bit of a hoot, I thought. Driving back from Aberspong on the Sunday morning, I was surprised to see everyone coming out of the little church at one o'clock!'

'Was that when it finished?'

'That's when they were all coming out. Was it a jumble sale or something?'

'On a Sunday? At the Catholics? I should think not. It was the confessional.'

'The what?'

'They all went to confession, even the Methodists. Then, they had to stay for the service so that it didn't look rude, and Father Umber preached hell fire and damnation for *hours* they said, he wouldn't stop, and they were all fed up and the children were frightened, and they were glad to get away AND IT WAS ALL MY FAULT!'

'Beloved, has there been any mass sinning in Aberbryncraig recently that I don't know about?'

'No, Stoopid,' this was more hopeful, 'they all thought that the Neptune Bar thief had owned up in the confessional and they might find out something if they went to church and it WAS ALL MY FAULT!'

'I don't see how it can be, beloved. What do you think you've done?'

'I started the rumour!' This made more sense. Mrs Mopalot was very capable of starting rumours, as her spouse well knew. He also knew that she might not have really done it. Rumours are quite good at starting themselves.

'Look beloved, just tell me what you think you've done and we'll have another cocoa with a slice of Neptune Bar in it this time.' Mr M was missing his magazine.

'All I did was to say to Fanny Williams that someone might have confessed to one of the vicars and ministers that they were guilty of taking those choc bars.'

'Fanny the Washing? You must be crackers love. She's got the biggest mouth in Aberbryncraig!'

'I know, and she used it. She said ever so loud that it would be Father Umber's lot because he's the professional confessional. I know for a fact that Evans the Lifeboat was listening and Dai News, and worst of all, those four children who hang around the Emporium all the time. I knew it would be round the school by playtime, to all the parents by teatime, to all the neighbours and families by bedtime and it was!' Mrs Mopalot had a good grasp of the village telegraph.

'You can't blame yourself for that, beloved, you didn't intend her to pass it on as gossip, did you?'

'I didn't intend the queue outside Father Umber's church either, although I nearly went and joined it, but when I heard about the sermon, I was glad I didn't.'

'And you wouldn't have been here with my dinner on the hob if you had and I couldn't have given you a great big kiss, like this…'

He made up for the imagined missed kissing with enthusiasm and they forgot about the cocoa, with or without Neptune Choc Bar bits in it, thereby being completely original, as no one had ever forgotten to consume a Neptune Bar before, in or out of their cocoa.

They didn't even wonder for a second if there might have been a real confessional denouement or not, which was fortunate, as such speculation was a waste of time because the whole thing was a pair of dolphin socks.

Evans the Lifeboat Picks Up the Lifeboat Collection Boxes

Evans the Lifeboat

There were not nearly enough shops in Aberbryncraig willing to have the Lifeboat Collection Box on their counters. In fact, there were only four. It's not that the people were mean, they simply didn't want the extra hassle. The Aberbryncraig lazy gene came to the fore with a vengeance. It was useless to say, in order to persuade them, that the lifeboat box wouldn't be in the way, because they knew it wouldn't. It would be stowed on the shelf at the back in a trice unless it fell on the floor, accidentally of course, and got trodden into the rush matting, then swept up apologetically in the evening. They all thought it was more honest to be straightforward and say they wouldn't have one. So, they said just that.

As it happened, the day after Dai News had been to see Dai Copper, Mr A Evans – Lifeboat man of this parish (no one knew what the 'A' stood for, so he was known as Evans the Boat) – who was in charge of fundraising, only had his remaining two boxes to collect and empty. One was in the *Heddlu* (frequently full of buttons) and the other one in Dai News' Emporium.

Dai the Boat went to the *Heddlu* first, to get it over with, and because he was afraid, they would close. The box was eventually run to earth in one of the lockers. It was empty.

'Oh, I am so sorry,' said Dai Copper, doing his best to wring his hands, 'I must have put it in there by accident!'

'But it isn't your locker,' stated the disappointed Lifeboat man, looking at the label, 'It's PC Williams' locker.'

'Well, I don't know!' he replied, but he did. He had been snogging PC Nerys Williams in the locker room shortly after the collection box had been delivered. Oops.

The box stayed put. On the counter now, of course.

Evans the Boat shuffled out sadly, crossed the road, and pushed open the door of the Emporium. He collected the box from its place next to the Neptune Choc Bar display. It was surprisingly, and hopefully, heavy. Somewhat cheered, Ev bid Dai farewell and hurried off to open the box at the Lifeboat shack.

First of all, he had to persuade someone to witness him opening it.

The Vicar was wandering along the High Street, whistling. Correctly assuming that this esteemed gentleman had little, if anything, to do, at the moment Evans the Boat accosted him.

It took a matter of moments, to get the box open and the contents tipped out. Wondering if it might be a collection of particularly heavy buttons, Dai stared. It wasn't, it was lots and lots of fifty ps.

Mouths agape, the two of them counted them. There were fifty. Fifty 50ps! Twenty-five pounds!

How odd. But how pleasing. Perhaps he might not have to do that pesky raffle now. Whoopee!

They went to the Bryn Arms for a celebratory pint.

Evans the Lifeboat Forgets

At this point, dear reader, it must be noted that when he collected the Lifeboat collection box from Dai News' Emporium, Mr A Evans the Lifeboat was so excited that he forgot to leave a new, empty, box behind for further collecting. As he went to the Bryn Arms to celebrate with the Vicar after finding twenty-five whole pounds had been collected, he *completely* forgot. He hiccupped home several hours later (the Vicar was in trouble too, as Mrs Vicar had burnt the supper waiting for him), and Ev never gave it another thought. Not one.

Evans the Lifeboat Chats with Mrs M

(L) Evans the Lifeboat and (R) Mrs Mopalot

Later that day, Mrs Mopalot was walking purposefully along the High Street and only occasionally stopping to look in the odd shop window, when she was accosted by Evans the Lifeboat. He had been singing and Mrs Mopalot had noticed the singing as she walked along and had realised who it was. Evans the Boat always sang, especially after a pint or two. Mostly people went into shops to buy things they didn't need, to get away from him. It wasn't that he sang out of tune, he was perfectly in tune, with himself, but he was simply sharp and loud and it grated.

Poised to go into the "Posh Paint: Ice cream in Forty Flavours and Knick Knacks" shop to escape, (not that she would ever buy anything *there*, but this was an emergency) Mrs M was hailed, mid-song, by the Lifeboat man.

'Hello Mrs Jenkins,' he said politely, stopping his singing, stopping in front of Mrs M and fortunately not starting to sing again, as he had more to say, 'if you don't mind my asking you, I wonder if you've got a spare moment for helping us out with a bit of a sweep round at the Lifeboat Station? We did have Fanny Williams but she wasn't as thorough as the Captain likes and anyway, she's got a new boyfriend with loads of dosh and she says she doesn't want the job anymore.'

Not over enamoured with being a replacement for Fanny Williams, Mrs Mopalot almost said she was too busy but remembering that her services weren't needed any more for poor Mrs Jones the Bins who had recently, sadly, passed away, gave her pause. Monday mornings, after the doctor's was finished, were now empty of work and the gas bill was due. These two things changed her mind.

'Is Monday mornings at about half past eleven any good, young man?' she asked.

'Perfect,' he said and the deal was done. Mrs Mopalot didn't know that this little (well not so little as she overdid it and cleaned the shed as well as the facilities) job would provide the beginning of the solution to the Great Neptune Choc Bar Mystery.

Who would have thought it?

Mrs M Has an Interesting Conversation with Evans the Lifeboat, Who Has Remembered His Omission

Mrs Mopalot was just hanging up her recently washed out nice, clean mop, head upwards so that it could dry, when Evans the Boat, who mercifully had not been singing, asked her politely if she would like a cup of tea before she departed.

As she wasn't expected at Father Umber's until after lunch, Mrs M said, 'Yes please,' and sat down on the little wooden chair that Mr Evans indicated.

Conversation was stilted until Mr Evans remembered that he had a favour to ask, and this caused a little frisson, although neither understood why. It was a very nondescript request.

He said, '

I wonder Mrs Jenkins, if you would do me a favour?'

'This is a nice cup of tea,' said Mrs M politely, then, 'of course, I will, Mr Evans, if I can.'

'Well, when I collected the Lifeboat Collection Box from Mr Edwards' Emporium,' he explained, 'I was so astounded by the weight of it that I forgot to leave an empty box to replace it. I wonder if I could ask you if you are going that way to your next appointment would you take it for me? Just pop it on the tall counter by the Neptune Bars if you would?'

'No problem at all, Mr Evans. I go past the shop on my way to Father Umber's.' Then she added, kindly, 'I'm glad the box was heavy when you collected it,' Mrs M was making conversation while she drank her tea. 'People aren't as generous as they used to be, I think.'

'Not in this case! There were fifty 50 pence pieces in the box!' said the Lifeboat man triumphantly. Something flashed in Mrs M's mind – a connection began. 'Twenty-five whole pounds!' he continued, then for honesty's sake, added, 'and two pennies and a button.'

'Fabulous!' appreciated Mrs Mopalot.

'It might let me off doing that pesky raffle,' finished Mr Evans. Mrs Mopalot knew he hated the raffle. No one ever donated any raffle-able prizes. Also no one bought any tickets. Perhaps doing it in the market square, when the market wasn't on, was a mistake.

Fifty *50 pence* making twenty-five pounds, though, thought Mrs Mopalot. What does that remind me of? It took her until bedtime to work out what it was.

Telling Stoopid (Sorry Mr Mopalot) About the Lifeboat Box

Mrs Mopalot slipped out of her corset. Well she wouldn't call it a corset, she called it a tummy shaper or some such fiction. Mr Mopalot called it a corset and got told off. She threw the offending garment on to the bed in exasperation and breathed in deeply, now that she could.

'I really have got some extra special news today!' she said with more breath than she'd had for some time, 'but I'm waiting until I've got into bed to tell you.' This last was slightly muffled, as a long, flannelette garment floated over Mrs Mopalot's head with a whoosh.

'I'm all agog, beloved,' lied Mr Mopalot, as he tried to read his railway magazine under the bedclothes, 'and mind your cocoa with your nighty.' This last was said just in time as his wife shook her nightdress down to her feet with a wriggle, missing her cocoa by a thousandth of an inch. She clambered into bed with a gusty sigh, settled herself down into her feather pillows and picked up her mug of cocoa.

'Right,' she said in preparation.

'Yes beloved?' the magazine went further under the counterpane than was strictly necessary, 'I'm all ears.'

'Well,' she began, 'I'm going to be cleaning for Evans the Boat now.'

'Good, beloved, I think you told me before beloved, and that's nice. Is that it?' He turned away.

'Not at all. I started today and crimbles but it needed doing. It was filthy under the boat.'

'You don't have to clean under the boat, surely!'

'Well no, I'm supposed to do the kitchen and the facilities but I had to have a good sweep first – so they won't walk any more dirt in when I've cleaned you see.'

'Is that what you wanted to tell me, beloved?'

'No, no, no. What I want to tell you is that I was talking to Evans the Boat while I was in there and you'll never guess what!'

'I probably won't, beloved. Why don't you tell me?' He hoped his exasperation wasn't showing. His wife lowered her voice to a whisper and went on, 'The Lifeboat box was collected last week and guess what was in it?'

'Buttons?'

'No.'

'Monopoly money?'

'No!'

'What then?'

'Fifty pence pieces!'

'Surely that's *good* beloved?'

'You don't get it. ONLY fifty pence pieces.'

'That *is* a trifle odd.' He turned a page of his magazine surreptitiously and concentrated on the article about painting model train carriages he was trying to read.

'Exactly.'

Mr M gave up on the article and said, 'What do you mean – exactly?'

'How much is a Neptune Choc Bar?'

'50p.'

'And how many Neptune Choc Bars has Dai News had stolen?'

'Fifty – so far. Are they still going missing?'

'They haven't had time to. It was only yesterday Dai went to the *Heddlu*, and, wait for it, there were fifty 50 pence in the box!!!'

A light bulb went on in Mr Mopalot's head. 'How many fifty pence were there in the box, did you say?'

'Fifty.'

'But that's how many Choc bars are missing.'

'That's how many Choc bars are missing.'

'Are you thinking what I'm thinking?'

'I'm thinking what you're thinking.'

They chorused,

'That's where the money for the Neptune Choc Bars went!' and Mrs Mopalot finished the sentence by adding, 'Into the Lifeboat box!'

They both burst into uncontrollable giggles and crashed their cocoa mugs together in celebration, making a few drops of cocoa fly onto the coverlet and Mr Mopalot's railway magazine. Neither of them cared.

Then Mr M put his usual damper on everything.

'We can't be sure,' said Mr Mopalot in a depressing voice. He had really thought he might be able to get back to his railway magazine soon but had to be honest.

'We can't be sure about what?' replied his wife.

'We can't be sure the two are connected.'

'You're going to tell me I need more evidence, aren't you?'

'Corroborative evidence, beloved.'

'More evidence.'

'Evidence that shores up your theory. After all, someone could be putting 50p into the Lifeboat box out of the goodness of their hearts. We can't assume it's for the Neptune Bars. It could be a coincidence.'

'It's some coincidence.'

'No, coincidences don't count. More evidence is needed to support the theory before we can be sure.'

'I see,' said Mrs Mopalot, somewhat deflated.

Then she squawked loudly, causing Mr Mopalot to jump and spill more cocoa,

'Oh no,' she said, 'I've just remembered, Evans the Boat asked me to take the new collecting box to Dai News. Only, I forgot it. I left it under the boat, actually. Oh, bother, I'll have to remember to go and get it. Someone will find it if they get a shout I suppose, but you can't ask them to take it to Dai News in an emergency, can you? Well, I'm not going for a day or two, I'm too busy.'

'I don't suppose it will matter, beloved.' But it did.

Mrs Mopalot Looks After
the Emporium

Dai News was just stocking his jar of humbugs up to the top again, as there had been a run on them the day before, when Mrs Mopalot let herself in with her key. It was half past six in the morning.

Dai News grunted a greeting and Mrs M grunted one back. She was only just awake. It wasn't a good time but Dai News' awkward angel decided to ask her a favour at that moment, mainly because he had to. There wasn't anyone else he could ask. It came out badly.

'Mrs Mop—er...Jenkins,' began Dai News.

'What?' Mrs Mopalot interrupted rudely.

Dai started again,

'Mrs Jenkins, I have a favour to ask of you. I hope you don't mind, but I wonder if you would mind the shop for me for an hour this morning?'

'It depends.'

'I have to go to the dentist for a big filling and I can't put it off any longer...' At this point Mrs Mopalot noticed the size of Dai News' face and its rather lurid colour. She hadn't looked at him since she'd come in. She frequently avoided looking at him as he usually appeared so cross. Her sympathy was ignited immediately. He looked awful. The need to go to the dentist was obviously acute.

'What time do you have to go out?' she asked, with a new sympathetic tone in her voice.

'Nine o'clock.' Dai News was having difficulty speaking.

'I'll come back then, I'll buzz off and do the Vicar now then I can stay in the shop for you. How long will you be gone, do you think?'

'About an hour they told me. I'll pay you extra.'

'That would be nice.'

And that's how Mrs Mopalot got to witness Mr Aled Jones' breakdown.

Mr Aled Jones Has a Fit

On that same day, Mrs Mopalot was dusting under the counter at Dai News' Emporium. As we know, she was cleaning and keeping the shop for Dai while he went to the dentist's for some urgent treatment. Very urgent treatment. Dai had a circular face the colour of a tomato.

So, she didn't notice straight away, that Mr Aled Jones had come into the shop, even though the little bell dinged on the door. The first thing she did notice, and was somewhat startled by, was his howl of anguish.

Mrs Mopalot stood up sharp and banged her head on the counter.

'What's the matter, Mr Jones?' she asked, quickly dashing round to the customer side to pat him comfortingly and remembering not to call him Mr Woolly Wobbly. He was speechless but pointed to the counter and sobbed.

When he gained a little control he wailed,

'It's gone. What can I do? I always have one! I don't know what I'm going to do without one! I can't bear it! What's the good of this?' he waved a fifty pence piece in the air, 'If it's gone, GONE!' And he beat his fist on the counter as if he might break the glass, sending the newspapers flying.

Mrs Mopalot's feeble 'What's gone?' was muffled as she tried to pick the papers up. Mr Jones sat down on the floor and beat his fists on it. Mrs Mopalot was seriously alarmed. She tried to get him to get up, but he was too heavy for her. She wondered if she should go over the road for Dai Copper.

Mr Jones sobbed on,

'Where's Dai News? Tell me where Dai News is. Is he in the back? Fetch him, will you, and be quick about it. He'll know. He'll know where it is.'

Mrs Mopalot told him that Dai News was at the dentist's with a face like a tomato. Mr Jones got himself to his feet, snorted enigmatically, then said, 'I'll be in tomorrow to see if it has come back, I don't suppose you know pig swill about it.' He stomped out and set off down the road to his bungalow.

Mrs Mopalot stood looking after him, dazed. Pig swill! She thought. *Cheeky man!* She'd forget to get the fluff out from under his bed if he wasn't careful.

Mr Aled Jones Is Upset About Not Having Had a Neptune Bar and Asks Mrs M to Get Him One

It was a wet and depressing morning and Mr Aled Jones hadn't bothered to get himself dressed or have any breakfast. He had only just left his bed for a cascading call of nature when he heard Mrs Mopalot's welcome key in the door followed by a warning toot on the doorbell. Mr Jones reflected that the toot should have come first and that Mrs Mopalot had got it wrong, but he so needed her help that he wouldn't have said anything for the world.

She marched in, all cleanliness and bustle. She had tussled with herself before setting off to Mr Jones's. He had been very rude the day before. He had been very upset too. Mrs M decided to put it behind her and maybe try to find out a little about what was the matter while doing his cleaning.

'Now, now Mr Jones,' she reproached, 'here's you being *dishabilled* again! We can't have this you know. I might be a married lady but I only like to see my Idwall in his jim-jams. Now be quick sharp and get your clothes on. Chop chop!'

Mr Jones didn't move. This was quite out of character and worried Mrs M had he had a seizure? Oops! No fun dealing with seizures. She was relieved when he opened his mouth and said in his best polite voice,

'Oh, Mrs Jenkins, I'm so sorry I said you didn't know pig swill about my little problem in the Emporium. You aren't the sort of person to be short of knowledge about pig swill,' he paused – this was going all the wrong way. –He started again. 'No, that's not it at all. I shouldn't have mentioned pig swill, not in front of a lady. What I'm trying to say is, I haven't had a Neptune Choc Bar for two days!!!' and at this point he burst into tears.

'Come, come,' said Mrs Mopalot, taking his arm and guiding him to a capacious, chintz-covered armchair in the sitting room and putting cushions behind his head. 'We can leave the dishabilled state for a bit, if you do up your dressing gown tighter. I'll make you a cup of tea and you can tell me all about it.'

'I don't want a cup of tea, I don't want a cup of coffee, I want my Neptune Bar!' He dissolved into sobs again.

'You might not want a cuppa but I do!' said Mrs Mopalot firmly and soon returned with two mugs and a big plate of biscuits, thinking that a hot drink and something to eat might help matters. It did. Quietly and gently, Mrs M got out of Mr Jones that he desperately wanted a Neptune Choc Bar but felt for some inexplicable reason he couldn't get one.

It seemed as if Mr Jones was saying she had to have a fifty pence piece Nothing else would do, so Mrs M firmly sorted him out,

'Look,' she said, 'give me 50p, no,' as he protested, 'any old 50p will do, five tens, ten fives, two twenties and a ten, it doesn't matter.' If she sounded as if she was trying to get a point across – she was, 'and I'll go and get you a Neptune Bar quick sharp, but make sure you're dressed decently when I get back.' Mr Jones looked up at her with something approaching adoration, mixed with amazement, and set off for a close encounter with his clothes, scratching his confused head.

'You can have a decent shave while you're at it!' Threw in Mrs Mopalot, as she opened the front door. She was right. Mr Jones looked as if he was a tramp who had come through a hedge, bum first.

'And it wouldn't be a bad idea to find a comb!' she added, as she opened the gate, although Mr Jones was pulling on his long johns; more cheerful than he'd been for two days and couldn't hear her.

That's how Mrs Mopalot got to have an extra job for Mr Jones every morning. It wasn't the end of it though, because now she knew a little about Mr Jones's confused ideas.

There Is No Lifeboat Box and Mr Wooly Wobbly, Mr Aled Jones, Doesn't Know Where to Put His 50p, so He Confides in Mrs M and Asks Her to Sneak It in the Next Day

It was a day full of confusion, although when she climbed out of bed and divested herself of her winceyette nighty, Mrs Mopalot was still unconfused and had done nothing but drink the cup of tea that Mr Mopalot had kindly provided before he set off for AberSpong at six thirty.

Everything was all right while she had her breakfast and as she set off for her first call of the day and stopped on her way for a few words with a neighbour in the High Street, the Vicar and a few others.

It was when she arrived at Mr Aled Jones' bungalow, (again) and handed over his Neptune Bar that the trouble started. This wasn't unusual. Mr Jones was a mine field, everyone knew that. It wasn't him being in his pyjamas that particular day, it wasn't him being obstreperous, (although he was) it was something he said. Well, some things he said, because there were several, and Mrs M began to wonder for his sanity. That is, until she began to put two and two together and made rather a lot.

When Mrs M arrived, Mr Jones was in the kitchen so, of course, he had to be thrown out of there so that she could get on. He would only get in the way and make everything take a lot longer otherwise. As he obediently went out through the door, his first odd utterance was:

'Can I have a word with you before you go, please, Mrs Jenkins?' Now this wasn't odd in itself, it was the way he said it. It was in the Neptune Choc Bar 'terrible worry' voice.

This voice had seemed to grow after Mr Jones's very disturbing (to him and to Mrs M) and inexplicable (to Mrs M) breakdown in the Emporium. It was a whining and babyish voice which reminded Mrs M forcibly of her youngest when he was a rather demanding two-year-old. It didn't suit a retired gentleman woolly wobbling to his dotage at all, but then perhaps it did.

The next thing happened when Mrs M had just about finished dusting the sitting room, cleaning the kitchen, having a cup of coffee, and vacuuming the hall but before she tackled Mr Jones's bedroom (always a big job) or the bathroom (worse). Mr Jones appeared and wheedled again,

'Haven't you finished yet Mrs Jenkins? Remember, I want a word with you before you go. Don't forget, will you?'

With determination, she finished the bathroom and was still hoping to get on with the rest when Mr Jones appeared again, '

Mrs Jenkins, would you come and talk to me now please? In case you forget and go home?'

So, she put down her cleaning things and followed Mr Jones into the sitting room. He sat down. She didn't.

'Oh, sit down for a moment Mrs Jenkins, please.' Mr Jones's voice had become worse. Mrs Mopalot sat.

'Now,' he continued, 'this is what I have to ask you.'

'Yes?'

'I wonder if you would make sure that you put the money in the right place when you get my Neptune Bar for me in the morning.'

Mrs Mopalot was mystified.

Mr Jones must have realised because he elucidated, '

I know it's difficult because the little box has gone away, but I'm sure you can do something, if anyone can. I don't know what Dai News is thinking of, you know, losing the box, but I'm sure you can find it if you look. With my leg, I haven't

76

been able to get to the Emporium, as you know Mrs Jenkins, since last week.'

What leg? thought Mrs M. She had assumed he was just too lazy to fetch his own Neptune Bar and so asked her to get it. *What's this about a leg?* She thought, but she said,

'Mr Jones, you're going to have to explain this to me. What box are you thinking of? Surely when you buy a Neptune Bar, you give Dai News, sorry, Mr Edwards, the money for it?'

'No, no, Mrs Jenkins, that's not what you do at all. I thought everyone knew, Evans the Lifeboat was very pleased when I got it right. You have to put the money for the Neptune Choc Bars in a Neptune Choc Bar box, it's right next to the Choc Bar display, only it's gone. I want you to find it and bring it back. I always put the money in there.'

Mrs Mopalot was confused, but not for long. Her eyes were as big as saucers as she realised the implications of it all.

'Oh, Mr Jones,' she said quietly, 'What shall we do with you?' And proceeded to try and explain but with little success.

The Mopalots Have a Think

Mr Mopalot (Idwall Jenkins as was) dropped his tool kit on the floor in the hall with some satisfaction and made his way into the kitchen to find his wife. He was startled to see she was very pink in the face and obviously rather wound up.

'Hello, beloved,' he began but she quickly talked over him.

'Idwall,' Mrs M blurted out, 'I've solved it! I know all about it! I'm so excited; I could go to bed right now!' Completely misunderstanding her, Mr M asked if he could take his boots off first.

'No, Stoopid, although perhaps…no, no, not just now, it's – we do all our detective work over our cocoa.'

Yes, while I'm trying to read, thought Mr M.

'It's a bit early for cocoa in bed and I want to tell you, but it's so comfortable in bed and we haven't had our tea and I am quite hungry and I can't wait any longer.' Mrs Mopalot was becoming incoherent.

Deftly summing up the situation and its possibilities, Mr Mopalot seized the moment, picked up two satsumas, two bananas and Mrs Mopalot, and made for the stairs.

When he had deposited his good lady on her side of the bed, and taken his position beside her he said,

'Right, beloved, out with it.' and he handed her a peeled orange.

Her husband's quick thinking – even though she had been transported unceremoniously upstairs and plonked in an undignified way into bed – calmed Mrs M and she began almost clearly now,

'I was at Mr Jones's today, and he was upset.'

'Again?'

'Yes again, but he made more sense this time – if you could call it sense I suppose.'

Mr Mopalot felt hooked. He had worked out that this might be something of importance, and he was now sure.

Mrs M continued, 'He told me a fantastic story.' *Thought as much* went through Mr Mopalot's head.

'He's been getting himself a Neptune Bar every day but he's been paying for it by putting a fifty pence piece in the Lifeboat Collection Box!'

Mr M couldn't contain his excitement:

#That explains Evans the Lifeboat's fifty pence pieces! That's your corroborative evidence!'

'There's clever.' said Mrs M sarkily. Mr M subsided.

Interrupted, but not stopped, Mrs M continued,

'So, when Mr Jones got to the Emporium the day before yesterday and had his fit,' she waited for effect, 'It was because there was no Lifeboat Box there and the silly little man thought if he couldn't put the money in the box, he couldn't have a Neptune Bar.'

'Good grief, that's well daft.'

'Tell me about it. He almost had Neptune Choc Bar withdrawal symptoms.' they both giggled, 'He was hysterical, saying he hadn't had a choc bar for two days and he couldn't cope. Today though, he wanted me to sort out the whereabouts of the box or smuggle a box into the shop so that he could get a Neptune Bar.'

'Is the poor old man losing his marbles?'

'No, I don't think so, he was always woolly, so Mum said, even at school, and he was seriously confused every Monday and Friday apparently. It was charming when he was young and good looking, or so I'm told, but any charm he's had has seriously worn off now. I had to walk all the way up to the Emporium yesterday, to get him a flipping Neptune Bar, and all the way back and it made me late for Evans the Lifeboat and the doctor. The doc was fed up with me because he's forgotten to give me a key and he had to wait in for me. He almost missed his drink at the Bryn with the Vicar and Father Umber. Now, I can pick a Neptune Bar up on my way past the Emporium. Saves me a lot of to-ing and fro-ing. Or he can even get it himself.' She took a deep breath after that lot. 'Once I've taken the lifeboat collection box round.' she gasped on the end with a sublime disregard for the complications caused by it all.

'Those three are a boozy lot.' Mr Mopalot was thinking of the clerical gentlemen and the doctor in the Bryn Arms.

'True.'

'It's good to know what's been going on though, isn't it, beloved?'

'I should say so, but what's to be done is a puzzler.' and with this Mrs Mopalot put the whole satsuma in her mouth at once.

'More corroborative evidence might help?'

In response, she did something horrid with Mr Mopalot's satsuma and he tickled her senseless.

Mrs Mopalot Finds 50 Neptune Choc Bar Wrappers in a Tin at Mr Aled Jones'

The 'The Vicar does a GOD job'

For once when Mrs Mopalot arrived at Mr Aled Jones' house, she found her employer so far from being dishabilled that he was completely dressed and in his best suit as well. She tried not to show her surprise, failed, handed over his Neptune Bar and said,

'Mr Jones, I am pleased to see you looking so smart! So early in the morning as well! Shall I put the kettle on? I think you might like a cuppa after all that effort.'

Mr Jones grunted a reply so she put the kettle on anyway, disappearing into the kitchen with her usual flurry and causing an immediate odour of bleach and soap flakes, followed by the whistling of the kettle.

'You go and have a sit-down Mr Jones,' she called out. 'I'll bring your tea in a moment or so.'

Mr Jones called back,

'I can't do that, Mrs Jenkins! I've got to go out. I'm going to the Vicar's new club for retired people and someone's picking me up in their car in five minutes.'

That's why he's up and dressed, is it? thought Mrs Mopalot. Well good, I'll be able to get on and get finished in good time if he's not here getting under my feet. So, she abandoned what she was doing, so that she could go and see Mr Jones off the premises, wiping her hands on her apron as she hurried towards the front door, where Mr Jones was anxiously waiting.

'Don't you fret, Mr Jones,' she said, 'I'll lock up right and tight when I go.' Just then, a tired-looking bright, blue car with THE VICAR DOES A **GOD** JOB emblazoned on the side and several passengers and Mrs Vicar's dog already squashed in it, stopped at Mr Jones's front gate and Mrs Vicar got out.

'You mind you do lock up,' said Mr Jones as he began to woolly wobble along his front path. Mrs Mopalot waved to Mrs Vicar and thankfully shut the door, thinking she would start in Mr Jones's bedroom. As he was not there to get in her way in the most untidy and grubby place in the bungalow, she thought it was a good time to remove the fluff from under the bed. Mr Jones usually objected to that.

She had a good dust round, folded up a few clothes and put all the ones on the floor into the dirty linen basket for Fanny Williams to wash. Then, she fitted the fat nozzle on to the hose of the vacuum cleaner and half kneeling, had a go at the under the bed fluff. It wasn't long before there was a metallic, crunching sound and she switched off the motor double quick.

'I was pretty sure there was nothing under there after I got the old shoes and that plastic bag out,' she said to herself, pulling the hose from under the bed. She was surprised to find an old tin of the famously inedible – but beloved by tough fishermen on cold nights – Cough Cough Cough drops wedged in the end of it. She gripped it tightly and pulled. She got it out but it opened and spilled…not Cough Cough Cough drops all over the floor, but blue, blue, blue Neptune Choc Bar wrappers. Lots of them. Lots and lots of them. Buoyed up by a sense of a ridiculous and vibrant curiosity, Mrs Mopalot counted the wrappers and was less than surprised to find that there were fifty of them. She began to look forward to bedtime.

Stoopid Finds Out That Mr Jones Hoards Neptune Bar Wrappers

Mr and Mrs Mopalot Jenkins were later than usual going to bed. There had been an old episode of *"Killings in a Welsh Winter"* on BBC Wales and they had both gone to sleep on the sofa. So, although it was now half past eleven, neither of them was very tired. Mr Mopalot had made double cocoas which presaged a long read and in his wife's case, a long chat, before sleep would claim them again.

Contrary to her usual practice, Mrs Mopalot had almost forgotten about the news of Mr Jones's unusual collection of wrappers and was dozing over a magazine passed on to her by her next-door neighbour, who delivered such offerings over the fence in exchange for some old copies of Mr Mopalot's railway magazines. Mr Mopalot's magazines, of course, had to be returned again to be archived in the ever-growing piles in the loft. The ladies' magazines Mrs M received were donated on to the doctor's surgery waiting room. It was all very complicated.

This particular ladies' magazine wasn't very interesting so Mrs Mopalot's mind wandered and then snapped back with a twang as she remembered the morning at Mr Jones's bungalow.

Careful not to cause a cocoa shower, she turned to her husband, and controlling her excitement she remarked quite loudly, '

Idwall! Listen to this! There's been a breakthrough in the case! You'll never guess what I found this morning!'

Calling the discussion over Dai News' Neptune Bars and their disappearance (which was, he thought, taking up too much time and energy in the whole village), a 'case' seemed ridiculous. Keeping his own counsel about this and putting down his magazine with a sigh, Mr M lent an ear. Mrs Mopalot took a deep breath, and to give her words more emphasis raised her voice a notch:

'At Mr Jones's, when I was vacuuming under the bed, I found an important clue to the mystery.' Mr M waited.

'There was a Cough Cough Cough drops tin.'

'Not surprising,' muttered Mr Mopalot, 'There's one under our bed. I've got paper clips in it, I think. I finished the Cough Cough Cough drops when I had that chest infection last year.'

'Ssshh!' continued Mrs M, but pausing for effect, 'In Mr Jones's tin, there were...' and she waited, took a fresh breath and then went on, 'fifty-three Neptune Choc Bar wrappers.'

'And in what way is this a monster breakthrough in your investigations?' Mr M applied his usual damper to proceedings.

'That's how many Neptune Bars are missing from Dai News' shop! There's fifty Dai had missing when he went to the Heddlu and three I got for him this week.' Mrs Mopalot's note of triumph faltered in the face of the look Mr M gave her.

'All that means,' said her spouse, 'is that Mr Jones has probably eaten fifty three Neptune Bars, probably in bed, and was too lazy to put the wrappers into the bin; he possibly didn't want to get out of bed in the cold, and so he put them in a tin, forgot about them until the next time and in the end couldn't be bothered at all. I may mention coincidences again here, beloved. Don't take them too seriously. It doesn't prove, in any way, that he stole them. Only that he had them. Your other corroborative evidence was better.'

Mrs Mopalot sniffed, and muttered to herself that she didn't say he stole them. She said he put the fifty 50p in the Lifeboat box. Looking at her husband crossly, (he was already back to his magazine), she turned over sulkily, and pretended to go to sleep, forgetting about her second cup of cocoa, which was still warm.

Mr Mopalot, seeing the error of his ways, put his magazine away under the bed with the Cough Cough Cough drops' tin of paper clips and snuggled down as well, gathering her up for a good squeeze. She forgave him instantly.

Flash Back: Myfanwy Decides to Give Mr Aled Jones a Neptune Bar for His Birthday

Seven weeks and four days before all this, well, fifty-five days before all this to be pernickety, little Myfanwy from the Junior school – best friends with Bethan and occasional cohort with Morgan and Owen – had a very generous idea. It was so very generous that it was quite unbelievable in one way. That way was 'why be nice to a grumpy old so and so who won't even say thank you?' but that was what Myfanwy was like. She was nice. Unfortunately, she learned from the experience and didn't do it again.

The children had seen Mr Aled Jones, you understand, walking on his own along the Promenade every day, as they ambled to school – the children were taking the short cut the long way round along by the beach, sometimes along the sands too – and then coming home the same way, and finding Mr Jones still there.

'I think he's lonely,' said Myfanwy.

'I think he's daft,' said Owen dismissively.

'What makes you think he's daft?'

'He's talking to himself. Anyway, everyone knows he's daft.'

'I don't,' Bethan chipped in, 'It's his birthday tomorrow, you know.'

'How do you know?'

'My nan went to school with him and she's got the same birthday. We're all going to a big party for Nan tomorrow. It has been years since she's had a party on the real day. She usually has to wait 'til Saturday.'

'Tomorrow is Saturday.'

'That explains it, then.' Bethan didn't care if she looked silly. She was very controlled and self-possessed. It was useful. She could turn on everything, from meek to furious at will, but was not so much as slightly shaken by either. She usually got her own way as a result. Myfanwy had an idea.

'I'm going to buy him a birthday present!' she declared. This was met with a chorus of:

'What with?'

'You must be as potty as he is!'

And

'Girls!'

Nevertheless, Myfanwy did buy Mr Jones a birthday present. It was a Neptune Choc Bar.

Picture the scene:

Mr Aled Jones was traversing the Promenade as he did every morning of his boring little life, when a small girl approached him, saying, 'Happy Birthday!' and presenting him with a thing in a blue wrapper with a mermaid and Neptune on the front, looking as if they were made of chocolate.

'What's this?' said the ungrateful, old curmudgeon.

'It's a birthday present, Mr Jones,' said Myfanwy politely. 'I know it's your birthday because it's the same day as Bethan's Nan's. She was in your class at school. Her name is Alice James, I think. Bethan says they used to get you mixed up because you've got the same initials as each other.'

'Oh, little Allie was it? And she's your friend's Grannie, is she?'

'That's right, Mr Jones.'

'See here, I don't want your present. Take it away now, take it away with you, now. It might be my birthday and it might not. I'm too busy to stop and talk anyhow. Go away!' and he tried to push the Choc Bar into Myfanwy's hands, but she stepped away from him and began to run, shouting back at him:

'Try it Mr Jones. You might like it!' and thinking 'I wish I'd put pepper on it, the miserable old thing.'

The fact was that Mr Jones did try it and did like it and was immediately hooked.

So the next morning, he set off to the Emporium to buy one for himself. He craved a Neptune Choc Bar with a passion.

Mr Aled Jones 'Buys' His First
Neptune Bar

The day after Myfanwy so generously gave Mr Aled Jones a Neptune Choc Bar for his birthday, using up a good half of her week's pocket money, Mr Jones – now deliciously hooked on Neptune Bars – set off first thing in the morning, not to the promenade as had been his habit, but the other way, towards the village and Dai News' Emporium of Newspapers and Sweetmeats. Mr Jones was looking to buy his first Neptune Bar.

He hurried along the road from the beach and scuttled along the High Street until he came to Dai News' Emporium. There was a long queue which reached the pavement outside. Dai News was flustered. Everyone wanted a different newspaper and several wanted sweets as well. One or two wanted Neptune Bars, so as soon as the part of the queue he was stuck in got into the shop, Mr Jones found out where the Neptune Bars were. On top of the cabinet. There was a brightly coloured blue box next to them which he could see was there to put your money in when you bought a Neptune Choc Bar.

All the Neptune Bars were in a big display box so you could help yourself. So as soon as he got on level with the Neptune Bars, he took one, looking carefully to see how much they were. Fifty pence! What a lot of money that was. Fortunately, he had a fifty pence piece, so he popped it into the box and the Neptune Bar into his pocket. It so happened that behind him in the queue was Evans the Boat.

'That's a good chap,' said Mr Evans approvingly, 'Better than all those pennies and halfpennies and buttons!' and he went off into a healthy guffaw of laughter. This little exchange stayed with Mr Jones.

The effect was, that he felt that he would be honour bound to only pay for his Neptune Bars with a fifty pence piece in the pretty box with a boat on it. He liked the picture of the blue sea on the box, like the blue on the beautiful, beautiful, delicious, mouth-watering Neptune Choc Bar wrappers. Of course, they had a boat with Neptune himself and a mermaid on their blue wrapper, but he could cope with the lack of that. He didn't know where to look when he encountered the mermaid's appendages.

When Mr Jones got to the counter, Dai News said in an exasperated voice, and slightly rudely,

'And what do you want?' as if somehow Mr Jones was unwelcome.

This caused Mr Jones's mind to go completely blank, so he said,

'A newspaper, please.'

'Which one?'

'The Sink please.'

The paper was handed over and Mr Jones had to find another seventy pence, much to his disgust. He wasn't to know, nor was anyone else, but the business with the Neptune Bars on that day was his undoing, and the undoing – in several differing ways – of the whole village.

Putting All the 'Evidence' Together; Totting It All Up

Mr and Mrs Mopalot met eye to eye over their cuppa, the one they always had after their evening meal.

'Are you thinking what I'm thinking, beloved?' enquired Mr M.

They found that thinking things at the same time often happened in their household. They didn't consider this phenomenon often, in fact hardly at all, but if they had, they would probably decide it was because they had been married for so long. Forty years and counting at that time.

'It depends if you are thinking we ought to sit down and look at all the evidence and decide what to do,' his wife answered, 'I know I think we should do that. It's difficult, what with people taking the mickey out of Dai News all the time, and him getting very upset, you know about that. If anyone else says "Look, write it down Dai, I *am* paying for this", there's going to be murder among the newspapers!'

'Then there's poor old Woolly Wobbly, as well you know too, he should be sorted out before something worse happens. He can't be left with all these delusions. It's not a good idea and no one knows what he will do next!'

'Goodness knows I have tried to explain to him!'

'I know you have, beloved but…'

'First of all,' suggested Mrs M, 'perhaps we should go for an early night? We're having our tea a bit late as it is, what with you not getting back from AberSpong until seven, and me not having the tea ready until eight, and it's nine o'clock now. Let's turn in and talk about it over cocoa like civilised people.'

Mr Mopalot couldn't argue with that. He was tired and also wondered if there might be a little 'Mopaloting' before the discussion, or even after it, if the talking didn't go on too long.

Ensconced among the feather pillows they enumerated the evidence. Mr Mopalot found a loose leaf in one of his magazines and wrote a list in the margin. It came out like this:

Mr Edwards is upset about the Neptune Bars being missing and not being paid for.

Dai Copper couldn't get the 'Serious Crime Squad' interested in choc bar theft and all the village was laughing and pulling Dai News' leg.

Dai News is losing his rag.

There is too much gossip and the clergy are being silly, praying and preaching sermons about it.

Mr Aled Woolly Wobbly Jones has been putting the money in the Lifeboat box instead of giving it to Dai News when he has a Neptune Bar, and he doesn't want to stop doing that because he thinks it's right (Evans the Boat said so!).

The money in the Lifeboat box really belongs to Dai News.

Evans the Boat won't want to give it back.

Mr Aled Jones (WW) has, in further evidence, got the wrappers, which came off the missing Neptune Bars, under his bed. Well, they probably are those wrappers. It's a bit of a coincidence if they're not.

At this point, the Mopalots felt rather weary and fed up with the whole thing.

'At least it doesn't look like a plot put into action just to be nasty to Dai News, beloved,' put in Mr M, 'That's the thing we were really worried about.'

'Thank goodness,' said Mrs M, but the "ness" part of the word was muffled under the bedclothes as Mr Mopalot decided she would be better off there. Sometime later, they surfaced and Mrs Mopalot suggested – and the suggestion was immediately taken up – that she should ask Mr Jones (WW) about the wrappers under his bed to clear up the last of the doubts. So, she did.

Mrs Mopalot Asks Mr Jones What Gives with the Neptune Bar Wrappers

Mrs Mopalot went to see Mr Aled Jones the next day. This was a mistake. He was alarmed. As is wasn't her "day", Mrs M didn't let herself into the bungalow, like she usually did, but she rang the bell and waited. This was the first confusion.

Then, because it wasn't Mrs Mopalot's "day", Mr Jones was embarrassed about the fact that he was dishabilled and at twelve o'clock too! This didn't usually bother him at all, but then it was normal in front of Mrs M when she was cleaning. It wasn't normal when Mrs Mopalot arrived unexpectedly and was then a visitor. No, definitely not.

So, he left her for an inordinate length of time while he not only addressed his clothes but put his best 'receiving visitors' suit on too.

In the circumstances, Mrs Mopalot didn't feel she could make herself a cup of tea while she waited either. It was all very tense, and boring.

Then Mr Jones decided he should make a cup of tea, which became interminable.

In the end, Mrs M gave up on protocol and descended on the kitchen and sorted him out, saying that she hadn't got all day and she only wanted to ask him something and how about going to sit down, and she didn't want a biscuit, thank you.

This was such a normal Mrs Mopalot way of being that Mr Jones was reassured and began to behave more as he usually did. That is, until Mrs M asked him about the wrappers under his bed.

His response was: 'And what were you doing under my bed?'

This unreasonable reply gave Mrs Mopalot pause, and she replied, carefully,

'Mr Jones, if you remember, I do your cleaning for you. That means I am expected to clean under things as well as on top of them.'

'Come off it!' re-joined Mr Jones a touch rudely, 'No one cleans UNDER a bed. That's daft. Nothing can get under there – the bed is on top. You shouldn't go looking under beds. It's none of your business. There's nothing there.'

'I assure you Mr Jones, that vast amounts of fluff can collect under a bed and everyone has to clean under their beds.'

'Fiddle,' he replied.

'Fiddle or not Mr Jones,' said Mrs M, who was quickly losing patience, 'I found a tin, I wasn't *looking* for it!' she had noticed Mr Jones's puce face. 'It got stuck in the nozzle of the vacuum,' Mr Jones cooled to orange, 'and it fell open and out popped fifty-three Neptune Bar wrappers.' Mr Jones heated up to puce again. In case he exploded, Mrs M got it over with quickly and said in a rush,

'Are those the wrappers from the Neptune Bars you got from Dai News? When you put the money in the little box?'

'What the pipe business is it of yours if they are?' This was the clearest sentence Mr Jones had constructed for some considerable time and Mrs Mopalot thought it sensible to assume it was the affirmative and depart. So, she did. She regretted going at all.

Mr and Mrs Mopalot Decide
What to Do and Do It

So it was time for the Mopalots to work out what to do.

There was further reason for this need in the fact that there were a lot of theories abroad about ways and means of solving Dai News' problem and most were bizarre and a few very worrying indeed.

For example, the Vicar, the Baptist Minister and Father Umber had started something they called a "prayer circle", which involved people praying more or less round the clock in the little Catholic Church. They were praying for help in finding the culprit. (Father Umber, much encouraged by his large congregation following the confessional debacle, was very keen on things happening in his church. He'd had three jumble sales, a coffee morning and had started a 'Young Mothers' group with a crèche already).

No one liked an unsolved crime. It reflected on the whole village, and Dai Copper was no use at all.

Some of the gossip was unkind, especially some started by Fanny Williams regarding Dai News' ability to run a newsagents' and keep track of his Neptune Bars. Most people knew that it was because Fanny had tried to get Dai News interested in herself and he had shied away, but it was nasty anyway.

Most of Dai's customers pulled his leg in one way or another, the mildest being, 'How's the Neptune Choc Bar count today, Dai?' It was driving him even pottier.

So it all had to be resolved – but how?

There was a long discussion over cocoa. Mr Mopalot even stowed his railway magazine in the po and gave Mrs Mopalot his full attention.

'The first thing we have to do is to tell everyone the truth,' she said, 'Mr Jones will have one of his fits, but that can't be helped. We have to stop the gossip. You know there's one theory that Dai News has hidden the Neptune Bars and is lying about it all because he's attention seeking?'

'I hadn't heard that one,' replied her husband. 'I have got an idea about how to get the news spread about, though. How about telling those children from the ysgol who hang about the Emporium all the time? Whatever they know seems to get about rather quickly.'

Mr Mopalot had obviously noted the efficiency of the Aberbryncraig telegraph.

'Now that *is* a good idea!' chimed in his wife, then she thought a bit and added, 'It would be good to say something about what could be done about it at the same time though. The main problem is getting the money back from Evans the Boat. He won't give it up, you know, because he doesn't want to do that raffle.'

This had them stumped for a while, then another light showed itself in Mr Mopalot's head.

'How about something simple?' he said, 'Like having a collection for Dai News, and giving any surplus to Evans the Boat, and then a big party? We could even do our own raffle with a Neptune Bar as the prize!'

'I tell you what,' Mrs M put in, 'I'll have a quick word in Annie Burford's ear, you know, that woman from the statics on the end of prom, she and her old man give those marvellous New Year parties, I bet she'd come up trumps.'

'You do that, beloved, and if she does come up trumps, tell those kids.' and with this Mrs Mopalot disappeared under the bedclothes with a gasp.

The Party

Needless to say Annie Burford did come up trumps and the children listened carefully to Mrs Mopalot, got most of it right, and told everyone in the playground at school, then told their parents and families at home, who told everyone else in the pub, the posh restaurants, the Mother's Union and over the fence, and soon everyone knew.

The clerical community gave up the prayer circle with some relief as they had been doing the praying during the small hours themselves as there were no volunteers for this and were tired and fed up.

The party – everyone was really keen on *that,* having been to the Burford's parties before – was to be held on the beach because there would be so many people (fortunately there was a heat wave expected) in a week's time, if enough money had been collected by then. Which of course, happened, as no one wanted to put the party off.

In the end, they amassed two hundred and forty pounds, three buttons with an extra forty-three pounds in Monopoly notes plus a piece of paper with 'one pound' written on it in rather a childish scrawl. When they had given Dai News his Neptune Bar money, and bought rather a lot of beer, the surplus went to the Lifeboat fund ('I won't need to do a raffle for ages!' said Evans the Boat).

Everyone stopped teasing Dai News' and Mr Aled Jones, rather than having a fit, became a kind of Woolly Wobbly hero. He might have caused the furore, but it was all rather amusing and he was taking it in his stride, jellyfish-walking about and eating Neptune Bars, still delivered by Mrs Mopalot, just to make sure that there was no reversion to putting the money in the Lifeboat box. The box was now tactfully on top of the newspapers on the counter just under Dai News' nose.

The party was a humongous success, with the local Barn Dance band playing (and being largely ignored) then a very loud disco run by Owen's brother, who did discos all the time and was rather good at it. It all went on well into the night and in some cases the next night too. The children were allowed to stay up late, and anyone too small to go to the party was tucked up in one of the many static caravans just behind the beach, while a rota of people stayed with them. This caused several small parties in the caravans too. Mr and Mrs Mopalot did the twist, and a bit of "Mopaloting" on the beach, behind the stones, Mr Aled Jones had too much to drink and went to sleep, jelly-fished out *under* one of the statics. He was found all right and put to bed in the caravan he'd been underneath, safe until morning.

Evans the Lifeboat was reeled in by Fanny Williams and no one saw him again for five days, while Dai Copper proposed to PC Nerys Williams (Fanny's sister) and was accepted. The announcement was made immediately by the inebriated but happy couple. This caused a hiatus in the party as everyone had to congratulate them and give them drinks.

Dai News was carried around on the shoulders of one of Mr Mopalot's beefier colleagues and everyone cheered as they were all well gone by then.

The food was amazing because everyone had pulled all the stops out and brought enough for twenty people each. The beer and lots of other alcohol, including a fair bit of homemade parsnip wine (lethal) flowed freely and frequently. Few people got over their headaches within the week.

The news of the party arrived in AberSpong two days later and the AberSpongites and sightseers missed it all. Even the after party.

Good.

Mr Aled Jones won the Neptune Bar in the raffle. Several people said the result was fixed.

(L) Fanny Williams and (R) Evans the Lifeboat

Mr Wooly Wobbly with the Neptune Bar.

Gillis 2021